SAM'S LIGHT

SAM'S LIGHT

Valerie Sherrard

A BOARDWALK BOOK
A MEMBER OF THE DUNDURN GROUP
TORONTO

Editor: Barry Jowett
Copy-Editor: Andrea Pruss
Design: Andrew Roberts
Printer: AGMV Marquis

Library and Archives Canada Cataloguing in Publication

Sherrard, Valerie
  Sam's light / Valerie Sherrard.

ISBN 1-55002-535-X

  I. Title.

PS8587.H3867S24 2004   jC813'.6   C2004-903135-X

1   2   3   4   5   08   07   06   05   04

  Canada

Conseil des Arts du Canada Canada Council for the Arts

ONTARIO ARTS COUNCIL
CONSEIL DES ARTS DE L'ONTARIO

We acknowledge the support of the **Canada Council for the Arts** and the **Ontario Arts Council** for our publishing program. We also acknowledge the financial support of the **Government of Canada** through the **Book Publishing Industry Development Program** and **The Association for the Export of Canadian Books**, and the **Government of Ontario** through the **Ontario Book Publishers Tax Credit** program, and the **Ontario Media Development Corporation's Ontario Book Initiative**.

Care has been taken to trace the ownership of copyright material used in this book. The author and the publisher welcome any information enabling them to rectify any references or credit in subsequent editions.

J. Kirk Howard, President

Printed and bound in Canada.
Printed on recycled paper.

www.dundurn.com

Dundurn Press
8 Market Street
Suite 200
Toronto, Ontario, Canada
M5E 1M6

Gazelle Book Services Limited
White Cross Mills
Hightown, Lancaster, England
LA1 4X5

Dundurn Press
2250 Military Road
Tonawanda NY
U.S.A. 14150

This book is dedicated to my son
Anthony Philip Vucenovic
with love,
pride, and admiration

Chapter One

My grandfather used to say that you never really knew a man until you worked for him.

"There's somethin' about having authority over another person that brings out a man's true colours," he'd tell me during some of our long walks through the woods behind his property. "I've had employers who'd sit up righteous-like in church on Sundays, who'd treat you like a friend out and around town. But you work for them and you see another side — a side that's mean and small. Then there are others you'd think would be hard to work for, and they'd turn out to be good men, and fair."

I'd listen as he told me about different bosses he'd had, and I'd take it all in, even though I'd heard a lot of it more than once before. I was never sure if Grandpa forgot he'd already told a story, or just thought it bore repeating. Either way, it really didn't matter. It was great when the two of us got to take walks and talk.

"You see, Cole, some folks don't understand that if you want a feller to respect and trust you, you've got to show him respect first. Another thing, you should never ask a man to do anything you wouldn't be willin' to do yourself. Back in '47, I worked for a feller who was known to be hard and tough, who expected a day and a half's work in a day. Thing was, he worked as hard as his men, and never raised his voice to any of us. Paid us fair for what we did too, considerin' the times.

"Some complained about the work and left, but I stayed on with him for six years. When your grandma passed on, he paid the whole cost. I didn't know a thing about it until I went to see the undertaker. Told him I needed to work out some kind of payment plan, so much a month until the bill was satisfied. With four kids to raise and barely enough money coming in to live on, times were mighty hard. Truth be told, I didn't know how I was going to manage even small payments. That was when he told me it was paid in full. Wouldn't say who'd done it, but I knew."

"Did you mention it to your boss?" I'd ask, even though I already knew the answer.

"I did so. Went right to his house to thank him that very day, but he denied it, and said maybe a person shouldn't be lookin' to thank anyone for something that was done anonymously. He said whoever had done it must have wanted it kept quiet. Said the best thing I could do would be not to say a word to a soul, and maybe help someone else someday when I was able."

He'd stop to light one of the cigars that my aunt Betty, who'd never married and still lived at home, wouldn't let him smoke in the house. Then he'd go on.

"I knew it was him all right, though. Wasn't anyone else around here would have done it. Thing was, with times being what they were, a man had little more than his word. A man's word was his honour, and it's all most of us had. What he did, in paying that bill, was make sure I could walk with my head up, and not have to worry that I hadn't been able to keep my word."

By the summer I'd turned fourteen, I must have heard about Grandpa's various jobs a half-dozen times. They were just some of the stories he told me, but the others weren't as important to me that particular year. After all, that was the year I got my first job.

I'd had my eye on a certain bike, a Kona Hardtail Stuff, but there was no way I could ask my folks to buy it. Mom gave up her job after my little sister, Jessie, was born. Jessie's in school now, but Mom hasn't shown any signs of wanting to go back to work. I think it's because she doesn't want to miss her dumb old soap operas.

My dad has a good job, so it's not like we're poor or anything, but we sure don't have money to throw around on an expensive bike.

Anyway, I decided to get a job and buy it myself. Well, that was easier said than done. Not a lot of places are looking to hire a fourteen-year-old. There was always a paper route, but I needed to make more than that paid or I'd be saving for the bike forever. I'd done some odd jobs the year before, mowing grass, cleaning out sheds, that sort of thing. That was okay, and most folks paid you fair enough, but it wasn't steady.

I'd asked at pretty well every store in town. When the owners found out I was only fourteen, they generally told me I was too young. Something about the law and child labour. Mrs. Cormier at The Mousetrap looked at me as if I was crazy.

"You're a *boy*," she pointed out, like that was some kind of crime.

"Yes'm," I answered, as politely as a person can when he's being stared at that way.

"You'd break things." She glanced nervously around the store, as if my very presence was a threat to all the junk piled on the shelves. The Mousetrap is a gift shop, and I suppose she thought of it as a classy place full of valuables. In fact, it's just a bunch of glass trinkets and stuff like they hand out for prizes in

Sunday School. Probably wasn't a thing in the whole place that was worth more than ten bucks.

"I'm pretty careful, ma'am," I insisted, even though I could see it was a waste of time.

"I'm sure you are," she said in a tone that clearly implied she thought I was lying through my teeth. "But I haven't any openings right now anyway."

She *could* have just said that right off.

It was discouraging, and I'd been almost ready to give up when I passed old Sam Kerrigan's shop. Actually, I guess I'd been walking past it every day while I searched for a job, but it had never occurred to me to apply there.

Sam isn't the kind of guy you'd call approachable. He's mean and surly, and rarely says more than a few words at a time. Grandpa used to say that Sam didn't have to be nice.

"Ain't a person in the county knows more than Sam does about small engines," he'd told me a few times. "He can practically fix somethin' by lookin' at it."

"Probably scares stuff into working," I'd answered once.

"Aw, Sam's all bark. I never heard of him doin' no one wrong, though he's bad-tempered enough all right."

Sam's Shop, which is actually the name of the place, carries all kinds of things that farmers and woods workers use, from chainsaws right down to twine for baling hay. It's so cluttered in there that you'd never find what you were looking for on your own, but Sam seems to know where everything was.

I hesitated at the door, telling myself it would be a waste of time to even ask him about a job. Then I screwed up my courage and went in anyway.

CHAPTER TWO

The door creaked when I pushed it open and stepped inside, which really added to my nervousness. I'd had it in the back of my mind that I could just slip right back out, without even talking to Sam, if I lost my nerve, but the darned noise made that impossible. It was always a bit gloomy in there, and I squinted for a few seconds while my eyes adjusted to the poor light.

Sam was sitting behind the counter, fumbling with some kind of strap, and I had a wild thought that he'd seen me coming and was going to tell me to hold my hand out for a whupping. He didn't glance up, though I knew he was aware of my presence.

"Good afternoon, Mr. Kerrigan," I finally squeezed out. My voice sounded funny, even to me.

No answer. Sam just kept working the strap, pulling it in and out of some sort of metal thing.

"My name's Cole Fennety, sir."

"So?"

"I've come to ask about a job." I exhaled hard once I'd got that out, relieved that it was almost over with. My guess was that he'd tell me to get lost, and right about then I was more than willing to do just that.

Sam finally looked over at me then, and the expression on his face wasn't what you'd call encouraging. It was a mixture of disbelief and disgust.

"How old are ya?"

"Fourteen, sir. But I'm willing to work real hard."

"What fer?"

The question confused me and I stood there feeling like an idiot and trying to figure out what he was actually asking.

"Whatcha want?" he asked after a few moments of awkward silence had passed.

"A job, sir." What I *really* wanted was to turn around and run out of there!

"What fer?"

"To earn some money."

"Fer what?" he asked, as though rephrasing the question would make it clear, even to one as obviously dumb as I was.

"For a bike." I swallowed, still not sure if that was what he wanted to know.

He grunted and went back to his strap. Another moment passed. I wondered what the heck I was doing there in the first place. I shifted from foot to foot.

"Fetch me a keel stick," he said suddenly.

The command took me by surprise, but I was relieved to have something to do besides stand there and feel stupid. I looked around until I saw the keel sticks. They were hanging on the wall behind him.

Half scared to get any closer, I walked nervously around the counter, reached up, and got one down.

"Put it back," he said.

I put it back, keenly aware that I was standing right beside the old guy, and that he was quite clearly off his rocker.

"Bring that Jonsered here."

The chainsaws were all displayed near the front window. I was only too glad to have an excuse to get away from him, even for a few seconds. As I passed the door, the urge to bolt out it nearly overcame me. I hesitated, but forced myself to go to the chainsaw section, pick up the Jonsered, and lug it to the counter. I stood there holding it, waiting.

"Put it back," he said, after what seemed like ten minutes had ticked by.

I put it back, but I was starting to get mad. It was obvious that he was just making a fool of me. When I turned to face Sam again, he was concentrating on the strap and didn't seem to have any more useless orders to issue. After a few more minutes had passed in silence, I figured I might as well just go.

I took one step toward the door, but my anger was growing and all of a sudden I didn't want to leave. As uncomfortable as I felt, I didn't want the old guy to see that he'd gotten the best of me. So, instead of walking out the door, I went about halfway across the floor toward him and just stood there.

Behind me, the door creaked, and in came Jeff Walker, a local farmer whose daughter Rhonda is in my class at school. They just live a few places down from my grandpa. He crossed the room quickly and spoke to Sam, who was still working on that darned strap.

"I need a spring for my tractor," he said. "As soon as you can get it."

Sam glanced at the broken part Jeff was holding in his hand and nodded toward the counter. Jeff dropped it there and turned to leave. That's pretty typical for transactions with Sam. Not a word from him. Jeff would know better than to even ask when the part might arrive, since all Sam would say would be something rude, like "When it does."

"Hey, Cole," Jeff greeted me as he passed. "How're your folks?"

"Fine, thanks."

"I bet you're glad to be out of school for the summer."

"Yeah, it's great." I never told anyone that I didn't really mind school. Some of the things we learn about history, especially wars, are pretty cool. Besides, it gets me away from Jessie's pestering, which is just about non-stop when we're at home. She's my sister and all, and I know she can't help doing weird girl stuff, but it's enough to get on a guy's nerves.

"Stop in next time you're at your grandfather's house," Jeff said. "Rhonda's always glad to have friends over. Summers are kind of long for her on the farm."

I said I'd do that, though I wasn't all that keen on the idea. Mainly, I didn't want Rhonda getting any dumb girl ideas. She's okay for a friend, I guess, but I sure wouldn't want her thinking I was interested in her or anything. Girls can get those notions like you wouldn't believe, and over the smallest things too. On the other hand, the Walkers have horses, and I sure didn't mind the idea of an afternoon of riding them.

Once Jeff had left I felt even more foolish to still be standing there. It seemed that Sam was finally finished with his strap contraption. At least, he laid it on the counter and walked over to a box of what seemed to be odds and ends. Rifling through the contents, he pulled out a long, round file.

"What's this?"

Since there was no one else there, I knew he must be talking to me, though he didn't look at me as he spoke.

"A chainsaw file," I said quickly. My grandpa filed his Husky with one lots of times, and had even let me do it once in a while, though I wasn't much good at it.

Sam grunted and walked into the back room without another word. Seemed ridiculous to stand there waiting for him to make a fool of me any longer. I decided to leave, and had reached the door when I heard him come back to into the store.

"Friday. Two o'clock," he said.

"I'm hired?" I could hardly believe it.

"Depends on Friday."

CHAPTER THREE

On the walk home I kept telling myself that it was great I'd gotten a job. Well, depending on Friday, whatever that meant. I suppose I was partly happy about it, but to be perfectly honest, I was more nervous than anything. Working for old Sam Kerrigan wasn't going to be a happy experience, that was for sure.

It had only been desperation to get a job so I could save up for my bike that had made me go in there at all. I hadn't thought for one minute that he might actually hire me.

One thing was certain: What Grandpa always said, about not really knowing a man until you work for him, didn't apply in this case. Everyone in town knew Sam was mean and hateful.

I'll just work hard and do my best, I told myself. If things worked out, I could get through one summer with him, for the sake of the Kona.

When I reached our bungalow, which looks like most of the houses on our street along the outskirts of town, I was looking forward to spending a little time working on my model. It's a level-five racer that I got for grading this year, and it would take hours and hours to finish. Not the sissy kind that you just snap together and don't even have to paint.

"Col-ee! Come here."

Jessie was out back, but she'd spied me coming up the sidewalk and was headed toward me, with a doll hanging at her side.

"I've told you before to stop calling me that," I said.

She smirked, the way she does when she knows she's getting under my skin. "Me and Penelope need a push on the swing."

"I'm busy."

"Come on. We *need* a push, don't we Penelope?" She held the doll up and wiggled it so its stupid head bobbed up and down, as if that would help convince me.

"No. Get lost, Jessie."

I ignored the fuss she set up and went into the kitchen. The TV was on in the other room, and I knew there was going to be trouble when Jessie came charging through the kitchen, howling.

"Cole is being *mean* to me and Penelope," she sobbed to Mom.

"Quiet, Jessie. I can't hear my show."

"He won't push us and we *need* a push," Jessie went right on, as though Mom hadn't shushed her. "We *need* one!"

"Cole! Be nice to your sister," Mom yelled. "There now, run along and play, dear. Cole's going to push you."

Jessie stomped back through the kitchen with a big, gloating smile on her face. "Mom says you *have* to push me and Penelope."

I felt like smashing her dumb doll's head in, especially after Jessie flounced back out the door chanting, "Cole's in trouble, Cole's in trouble." The only thing that stopped me was knowing it would be reported right back to Mom, and I'd end up grounded or something.

It's not fair, the way Jessie gets away with stuff like that all the time. Especially when Mom's watching those stupid soap operas! Jessie knows all she has to do is run to her and start blubbering, and Mom will take her side just to shut her up so she can hear the TV.

I followed the little brat outside, wondering how my best friend, Wayne, can stand living with four sisters when I can barely keep myself sane with one. It's no wonder we spend most of our time hanging out at the old quarry or, in the wintertime, at The Junction. That's a rec centre the town built for the teens a few years ago, and it has some cool things to do, like play pool or shoot baskets. Only problem is, there's always a bunch of giggling girls there, and they hang around watching the guys and just generally being a pain.

"Penelope doesn't like to go too high," Jessie announced once she'd gotten herself seated on the swing.

Is that so, I thought. *Too bad for her then*. I started out slow and easy until I had a rhythm going and then pushed harder and harder until the swing was cutting a half-circle arc through the air. It was time my sister learned a lesson!

"Wheeeee!" Jessie shrieked in obvious delight.

I'd been suckered! I could hardly believe I'd fallen for it. When the swing got close again, I shoved it hard on one side, making it lurch and wobble as it flew upward. Then I stood back fantasizing about Jessie crashing to the ground and busting up that dumb doll. Of course, there was always the chance that Jessie could hurt herself, too. Not that I much cared if she did, but it would mean big trouble for me.

"Hey!"

I turned to see Dad standing there watching. He didn't look too pleased, and I could tell he was about to launch into a big lecture about how my sister is just a little girl and I should be more mature and stuff.

Before he could say anything, though, I felt a sudden blow and went sprawling to the ground. The swing had come back while I was looking the other way, and Jessie's leg had slammed into the side of my head.

"OW!" Jessie yelled. "My leg!"

Dad had crossed the yard in a few quick strides and he grabbed the swing to get it stopped, then knelt down to check on me.

"You okay, son?"

"Yeah." I scrambled to my feet and watched as Jessie hopped around the yard on one leg, screeching the whole time.

"Let me check your leg, Jess," Dad said.

"It's broke! Cole broke it." She shot an accusing look at me.

Dad felt it and assured her that it was all right. She howled for another minute or so, and then switched to walking around with a ridiculous, exaggerated limp.

"Cole broke my leg," she announced to Mom as soon as we'd gone into the house. "He did it on purpose too."

"You can't walk on a broken leg," Mom pointed out. Her soaps were over and she was in the kitchen putting pork chops in a frying pan.

"Well, it's cracked for sure," Jessie said sullenly.

"Don't be such a retard," I told her.

"Cole," Dad gave me a warning look. "Don't speak to your sister like that."

"Well, she *is*," I muttered under my breath.

"Cole whispered something. I think it was a bad word."

"You two stop it," Mom said mildly. Most of the time, she stays pretty calm when Jessie and I are fighting, but once in a while she gets really mad and yells. Then we both get sent to our rooms. "Go wash up and come set the table for dinner."

I'd been planning to tell my folks about the job at Sam's Shop while we were eating, but at the last minute I changed my mind. After all, if things didn't work out on Friday, Jessie would have a field day telling everyone in town that I'd been fired after one day on the job.

Chapter Four

Wayne came by after we'd eaten and sat in the kitchen while I did the dishes. He never does stuff like that at his place.

"My sisters complained that it wasn't fair that I don't take a turn with dishes," he'd told me once, while I was elbow-deep in soapy water. "So Mom got on this big kick about everyone doing a fair share, and started to make me."

I had been a bit surprised at that, since I've never seen Wayne wash a single dish, or do anything else around the house for that matter, and I've been at his place lots.

"I outsmarted them all," he'd said proudly, after a pause. "I just made sure that they were only half clean. Mom couldn't take it. She'd stand over me and pass them back. I'd just half-swipe them and put them in the tray again — still dirty. She finally gave up and said I could do other chores instead."

"Like what?"

"Oh, I take the garbage out sometimes," he'd grinned. "Turns out that's the only thing I can do right."

That Wayne sure can think things up! I had to admire the devious way he'd managed to avoid helping around the house, but there was no way that kind of stunt would work for me.

Something else he's really good at is handling my annoying sister. I guess that comes from all the practice he gets with four of his own. Things that work for him never seem successful when I try them, though.

Today, for example, Jessie was sweeping the floor when he first got there. She was being her usual aggravating self, knocking the broom against my feet and then pretending it was an accident.

I ignored this, knowing full well she was just trying to get me going. Another fight and there was a good chance that Mom would drag the two of us into the living room and do one of her insane parenting things, like make us say nice things about each other. She does weird stuff like that once in a while, as if it will make us start getting along better.

So, there she is, bumping me with the broom, and Wayne comes in and starts staring at her. She can only stand it for a minute or so before she turns to him.

"What are *you* looking at?" she demanded.

"I was just noticing that you're not very good at that," he said innocently. "You're pretty clumsy for a girl, huh?"

"Am *not*," she sniffed, but that was the end of the assault on my feet. She finished sweeping without touching me again and then flounced out of the room, forgetting all about her limp.

When the dishes were done, Wayne and I headed out to the quarry. We stopped at a corner store to pick up some Pepsi and a couple of snacks for later. Angie Murdoch was working behind the counter. When we first went in she had her nose stuck in a book, and she laid it aside with a big sigh when we got to the cash register, as if we had no business disturbing her.

Angie is a couple of years older than us, and real pretty. She knows it too.

"Whatcha reading?" Wayne asked, leaning across the counter.

"A book." She slipped it out of sight on a shelf, like it was some big secret, and tossed her dark hair back with one hand. Angie is always tossing her hair back.

"Yeah? Any love scenes in it?" Wayne asked. Before she could answer he added, "You and me should make some love scenes of our own sometime."

"Don't be such a pig, Wayne." Angie scowled and started to ring in our stuff.

Wayne made loud kissing sounds, which she ignored. We paid up and headed for the door. Wayne stopped in the doorway, spun around, and pointed at her like Austin Powers.

"You *know* you want me," he said, just before we stepped outside.

She was already picking her book up again, but she paused and put a finger in her mouth in a gagging motion.

Wayne burst out laughing as we walked away.

"I don't know why you do that," I said. "She already thinks she's so hot that every guy in town is after her. Why feed her ego?"

"'Cause you just never know, Cole." Wayne looked off into space. "You just never know."

Wayne likes to say that he's hedging his bets when he pulls some stunt like that. Insurance for the time he might need it. I think it's ridiculous. Angie would never be interested in someone our age. She goes out with a grade-twelve jock on the hockey team, and he has a car and all. Besides, who'd want a stuck-up girl like that around?

I let it drop, though. No point getting into an argument over someone like Angie when I had big news to tell him. I'd already decided to wait until we got to the quarry before I filled him in on my job at Sam's.

The quarry is a big pit at the end of a field that stretches out behind the machine works building. The road back to it is overgrown now, and hardly wide enough for a small car to drive along, though it used to be travelled by dump trucks.

I like going through the field myself, but one time last summer Wayne stepped on a snake there and screamed like a girl. It was pretty funny, but I didn't hardly laugh at all 'cause Wayne's not what you'd call much of a good sport when a joke's on him. He insisted that he was just startled, and that he's not scared of snakes, but I noticed that he always wanted to take the road after that.

We reached the quarry and went right to our usual rocks, a group of huge boulders along the west side. Most of the time we just sit there and talk, or sprawl over them and let the sun beat down on us. It's real peaceful, with woods stretching out beyond the pit, and sometimes we see a few deer or smaller animals at the edge of the forest.

When I'm alone, I like to take a walk into the woods, until I get to the river that runs along the north side of town. Wayne doesn't much like the woods. He says it's because he doesn't want branches ripping his clothes, but the truth is he's nervous of bears. I've only seen a bear there once, and it just looked at me and disappeared into the brush. It was a mistake to mention it to Wayne, 'cause it was right after that that he developed this sudden worry about his clothes.

I guess this all makes him sound kind of cowardly, but that's not true. Wayne has never backed down from anyone in his life. He'd stand up to the biggest, meanest guy at school without batting an eye, and if that means fighting him, he's up for that too. It's just certain things that make him nervous.

We'd settled into our usual places this day, and my chance to tell him about Sam's came up pretty quick.

"We should think of something to do this year, instead of just hanging around here all summer," Wayne said. "It would be cool to go somewhere, if we can talk our folks into it. I have an uncle in Toronto, and he'd probably let us stay there for a few weeks."

I could practically guarantee you that my parents wouldn't be packing me off to Toronto without them, so I was glad I had an excuse.

"Sounds good," I said, "only I got a job today."

"Yeah?" He didn't look all that happy to hear it. I'd told him I was looking for work, but he'd said right from the start that it was a waste of time. "Where?"

"At Sam's Shop. I start on Friday." I filled him in on my visit to Sam's.

"So, it's just a tryout then. Even if he doesn't fire you, which he probably will, you'll never last working for that old grouch." Wayne shrugged, as if that settled it. "I say we start wearing our folks down now, and then by the end of July, we'll have them persuaded to let us go to Toronto."

"Okay, sure." I tried to sound enthusiastic, but the truth was I was kind of put out, the way he just assumed the job wasn't going to work out for me.

That might just have been because he was echoing my own thoughts.

CHAPTER FIVE

Friday came, and I was as nervous as a mouse thrown into a roomful of cats. I woke up early, and the hours I had to put in until two o'clock ticked by slower than usual. It was like when I've done something wrong and I'm waiting for my dad to get home and find out about it.

Jessie seemed to sense that this was a good day to bug me. She did everything possible to get on my nerves, which wasn't much of a challenge, considering they were already on edge. I thought briefly about doing something to trick her, like I did last summer when I told her we were going to play hostage and tied her to the oak tree in our backyard. I'd left her there then, and gone off for the day.

Turned out Mom didn't notice her yelling for a while, which was no big surprise, seeing as how Jessie sets up a fuss over absolutely nothing on a regular basis. I'd been grounded for a week that time, but it was worth it.

Well, I already had to come up with a story to cover me for the time I'd be at Sam's. There was no need to complicate it by getting myself in trouble over my stupid sister. The big worry was that I didn't know how long Sam would want me to stay. He'd said two o'clock, but hadn't mentioned what time I'd be getting off. The shop is open until nine on Friday, so it was possible he'd want me to stay until closing.

I considered saying I was going to Wayne's and might stay for supper, but there was always a chance Mom might call there for some reason. Lying is a big deal in our house, and if I got caught, I'd be in a heap of trouble.

In the end, I decided to tell her that Sam had asked me to give him a hand for the day. Then, if the job didn't work out, I wouldn't lose face by having to admit I was fired. I did that right after lunch, just as Mom's soaps were coming on. That's the best time to slip something by her without too many questions, since she's concentrating on the TV.

She nodded and waved me away with her hand. I wasn't entirely sure that she'd heard what I'd told her, but that was okay, since Jessie was standing behind me in the doorway, being nosey, as usual.

"You got a job?" she asked, following me through the kitchen.

"I'm just helping him out for today."

"How much you gonna get paid?"

"I don't know, whatever he gives me." That was another thing Sam hadn't mentioned, but it was a safe bet he'd give me a lot less than he'd have to pay someone who was over sixteen. There was no hope for minimum wage, but whatever I got would be better than nothing. Besides, if the job worked out and I didn't like the rate, I could always quit.

Jessie was looking at me weird by then, and it was a shock to realize that she was impressed.

"Cool," she said. "I'm gonna get a job when I'm fourteen too."

I was about to say, "Who'd hire you, you annoying little geek?" but I stopped myself. Instead, I told her she probably would. After all, she seemed pleased for me, which was more than I'd gotten from my best friend.

"What kind of stuff will you be doing?"

"He'll tell me when I get there." I waited for the onslaught of more questions, but she went off to another part of the house.

A moment later, she came back and held out her hand. There was a stone in it, about the size of cherry. It was white quartz with yellow veins.

"You can take my lucky rock with you," she announced grandly. "But just this time, and don't lose it."

I caught myself before I could ask why I'd want her dumb old rock. "I'll put it in my pocket," I said. "That way it can't get lost. Uh, thanks."

"Hey, you want me and Penelope to visit you at work?"

"No!" I blurted. The hopeful smile faded from her face. "I mean, bosses don't like it when their employees get personal visits or phone calls."

It was too late. She'd seen how horrified I was at the thought of her coming into Sam's Shop, and wasn't fooled.

"Give me back my rock," she demanded, hand outstretched. "You're mean."

I gave her back the rock and waited for the usual outburst, but it didn't come. She took it and walked slowly back down the hall to her room. She looked real small.

It was almost time to go to Sam's, and I decided to leave a bit early. Not because I felt guilty about Jessie. After all, her main goal in life is to torture me. Why should I feel bad just because she was acting like an actual human being for a few minutes? I suppose, though, that it wouldn't have killed me to say I was sorry.

It was quarter to two when I got to Sam's. I went in and found him sitting behind the counter fiddling with some sort of small motor.

"Mr. Kerrigan," I said when a moment had passed and he hadn't spoken. "I'm here."

"I figured that," he snapped, "when I saw you standing there."

"Yes, sir."

"You come to work, or stand around?"

"What would you like me to do?"

"Shipment's coming soon. You can put it away. Clean til then."

The shop looked like it had never been cleaned since it was first opened. Looking at the clutter and dirt that surrounded me, I reminded myself that this was my only shot to get the Kona.

"Where are the cleaning supplies?" I asked, doubtful that there were any.

Sam jerked his head toward the back room. I walked past him and found that the room in behind was even worse than the shop. It took me a few minutes to locate a mop, broom, bucket, and sponges out there. A bottle of all-purpose cleaner was in the bucket, and it was no surprise to me that it was full.

I filled the bucket with hot water, added some cleaner, and lugged it out to the front. Clearing small sections of the shelves that ran down the middle of the room, I washed them, wiped down the hodgepodge of things stored there, and replaced them as neatly as possible. It took me nearly an hour to finish the first two shelves.

By then, the shipment had arrived. The delivery man had obviously been there before, since he just brought in the boxes, presented Sam with a paper to sign, and left without bothering to make conversation.

I tore the packing tape from the boxes and started putting the stuff where it seemed to go. The shop was divided into sections for farming and woods supplies, sorted by size. When I came to items that weren't familiar to me, I had to ask Sam which section they went into. Each time, he looked at me as though I was an idiot, and stabbed a finger in the right direction.

Then I came to a box full of unrelated odds and ends. I picked a few of the things out and was about to put them on the shelves when I spied a spring in there.

"I think this must be parts for repairs, or that you've ordered in for folks," I said, lugging the box to the counter.

Sam seemed startled. He stopped what he was doing and pawed through the box.

"Why'd ya think that?"

"I saw Jeff Walker's spring there, the one he ordered when I was here the other day."

Sam grunted.

"Do you have a list of customer orders?" I asked. "If you want, I can call folks to let them know their things have arrived."

Sam reached under the counter and pulled out a book that had orders written in it. He tossed it toward me. I got out the phone book and called the names on the list as I located each item in the box.

CHAPTER SIX

By the time six o'clock came I was getting real tired. I'd managed to get everything put away, and had cleaned a few more shelves, but by then my arms were starting to get sore. Every once in a while I wondered how much Sam was going to pay me an hour, and if it was going to be worth it.

I suppose I could have come right out and asked him, but the thought of how he'd respond kept me from opening my mouth. There was no conversation between us, though a few customers spoke to me as they came in to make purchases or bring things in to be repaired.

I was surprised at how many repairs there were, and how fast Sam seemed to be able to get things done, for all that he appeared to be working at a snail's pace. He'd bring something out to the counter and take it apart, and his actions would seem slow and clumsy.

Then the next thing I knew, it would be done and put back together and he'd be on to something else.

It was equally amazing how he knew exactly where to find the parts he needed. Most of those things were kept in the back room, and he'd disappear out there for a few seconds and then come back with what he needed, though how he found anything was beyond me. There were shelves and boxes and filing cabinets back there that seemed to hold a huge assortment of odds and ends in the most haphazard fashion possible. I guess Sam was used to it and had his own system of knowing where things were.

Aside from being tired and sore, I was getting hungry. It hadn't occurred to me to bring something along to eat, and to be perfectly honest, I never thought I'd be there for more than an hour or so before he'd let me go. Well, I figured I could last until nine if I had to, though I kept picturing my folks sitting down to a big meal, which was making me even hungrier. At least there was a sink out back, so I was able to get a drink of water when I got too thirsty.

Then six-thirty came, and Sam went into the back and came out with a loaf of bread and a chunk of bologna. He cut slices from it, slapped together a couple of sandwiches, and laid them on sheets of paper towel.

"Here," he grunted, pushing one sandwich toward me while he bit into the other. He squirted a bit of mustard onto the meat before each bite he took. I thought that was kind of odd, since he could have just put mustard on the whole thing at the first.

I picked up the sandwich he'd made me and took a bite. It was pretty boring, but I felt funny about opening it and putting mustard on it. It seemed that he might take that as some kind of criticism for the way he was eating. So, instead, I squirted a little blob on each bite, the way he was doing.

Maybe it was because I was so hungry, but it seemed to me that it was the best bologna sandwich I'd ever eaten. I decided that Sam's method might have something to it, and that the mustard had more tang and flavour when it was put on that way.

"Nuther?" he asked, when we'd swallowed the last bites.

"Yeah, thanks."

He went through the ritual again, spreading slices of bread out and cutting the bologna onto them. By the time I'd eaten the second sandwich, I was full, and feeling a lot better.

Sam wrapped up the remaining meat and took everything back to the fridge in the other room. I went back to work on my cleaning.

The next few hours went by pretty fast, and by the time nine o'clock came, I'd finished the whole middle section of shelves. Still, considering the dirt and disarray in the place, it didn't seem much of an improvement.

Sam put down the chainsaw he was working on and lumbered over to the door, turning the sign around so that the side that said "Closed" was facing out. He looked at me for a long minute, as though he was trying to figure out who I was and what I was doing there.

"We're closed," he said, as if I was a customer.

I put the bucket and sponge away. Then I gathered my courage and asked Sam if I had the job or not. He seemed to ponder this before handing me a folded piece of paper and shooing me out the door.

I went down the street a ways, until I was out of sight of the shop. Stopping under a streetlight, I opened the paper. On the top was written, "Cole Fennety's Schedule." Underneath, in a column that was neatly centered on the page, was a list of shifts for the whole next month.

"Yes!" I whooped, thrusting a fist into the air. Today hadn't been as bad as I'd thought it would be. I figured it wouldn't kill me to put up with Sam's grouchiness for the summer.

Looking closer at the list, I was surprised to see that today's shift was there. Somehow, I'd thought he must have done up the schedule while I was working, but it seemed he'd already had it written out before I started. Of course, that didn't mean anything. If he'd decided not to keep me on, all he had to do was throw it out.

I saw that I was scheduled again from noon to six the next day. At least I'd know how long I'd be there each day, and whether or not to bring something to eat. I didn't suppose Sam would expect to feed me every time I was there.

A quick calculation of each week's shifts told me I was going to be working pretty much full-time. It would be a great start toward saving up for my bike.

I happened to glance back toward the shop then, and saw Sam standing out on the sidewalk, looking in my direction. I felt a bit foolish, and wondered if he'd seen my reaction when I'd first opened the page. *Well*, I thought, *no sense in letting that bother me.*

On impulse, I gave Sam a wave and shouted, "See you tomorrow."

Naturally, he just turned around and walked off without a word.

CHAPTER SEVEN

Now that the job looked pretty solid, I could harldy wait to tell my folks all about it. I hurried home, walking along Water Street, turning on Green, and crossing through the elementary schoolyard to save time in getting to Howard Avenue, where our house is.

Our place is like most of the homes in Kesno, a three-bedroom bungalow with white siding. There are only two areas of town that have fancier houses. One is a newly developed section near the outskirts, where doctors and lawyers and men who work in management at the mills live. The other is in the older part of town, where the houses are big and old-fashioned, most of them three storeys high, with pillars and huge verandas. A lot of them have been converted into apartments or duplexes though, and some are getting kind of run-down.

Kesno isn't a very big place. The main industries here are farming and products from the endless forests that surround the town and supply wood to the paper and lumber mills. My father works at the paper mill, which smells foul and makes his clothes stink. I don't know how anyone stands living near it, since the air around the mill always smells kind of like rotten eggs.

When I got home, Mom and Dad and Jessie were in the living room, watching *Milo and Otis*. That's one of Jessie's favourite movies. Grandpa gave it to her for Christmas a few years ago, and she still isn't sick of it. It's always amazing to me that my parents will sit down and watch it with her, and even act like they're enjoying it.

"Guess what," I said as soon as I was in the room.

"Shhhhhhh!" Jessie glared at me.

"I got a job," I said, keeping my voice casual.

"Make Cole be quiet. I can't hear."

"Cole, your sister is watching her movie," Mom said automatically. Then her head came up and she turned to look at me.

"Did you say you got a job?" Dad had reacted quicker, and was already getting to his feet.

"Yeah. At Sam's Shop."

"No kidding!" Dad whistled. "How'd this happen?"

"I went in the other day and asked him if he needed anyone, and he hired me."

"Jessie said you were helping him out today," Mom said, "but I had no idea it was for more than just one day."

She was coming at me then, and I knew by the look on her face that there'd be no escaping a hug. She grappled on to me and squeezed. I let her, even though I'm nearly a man and too old for that sort of thing.

"Can you believe it, Grant?" Mom said. "Our little boy, with his first job."

Dad smiled at me the way he does when we have to humour Mom. He shook my hand and told me he was real proud of me.

"Sam Kerrigan is a smart man, even if he is a bit rough around the edges," Dad said. "You'll learn a lot working for him."

I didn't bother telling him that all I was doing was cleaning the place and unpacking boxes. The chance that Sam would waste his time teaching me anything was about nil.

"I gave Cole my lucky rock but he was *mean* to me so I took it back," Jessie announced, looking up from the TV. She can't stand it when someone else is getting any attention.

"I'll be working pretty much full-time," I said, ignoring her.

"Me an' Penelope were going to visit him at work," she went on, "but we changed our minds because he was *mean*."

"Penelope and I," Dad corrected. "Full-time, eh, Cole? Well, that's great. You sure you won't mind spending so much of your summer working, though?"

"Nah. Wayne and I were thinking of taking a trip to Toronto for a few weeks, but I guess I'll have to tell him I won't be able to, now that I'm working and all."

"Wayne says bad words," Jessie said importantly. "He says things like …"

"Jessie," Mom cut her off quickly, "that will do."

"Well he *does*."

"What's this about a trip to Toronto, Cole?"

"Oh, nothing," I wished I hadn't brought it up. Why I did, I have no idea. It's not like I'd really thought I would be allowed to go or anything. "It was just an idea Wayne had."

"I wish you'd go to Trono an' *stay there*," Jessie said. "Then nobody would be *mean* to me an' Penelope."

"Now, Cole," Mom looked all worried. "You're far too young to be gallivanting about on your own. Why, any number of things could happen."

"It's a moot point, dear," Dad pointed out. "No need to get worked up about it."

"I am *not* getting worked up. I'm just saying he's too young."

"Well, since he's working, it's not even a consideration."

"Why, if Lucy had just listened to her mother, she wouldn't be in the mess she's in, trapped in a mountain cabin with that madman, Eduardo."

"Lucy *who*?" Dad asked.

"No one even knows where she is," Mom said vacantly. "Of course, she had to keep it secret since her mother forbade her to see Eduardo again."

"Then how do you …?" Dad stopped and stared at Mom. "Is this something from one of those soap operas, Joan?"

Mom looked startled. The glazed look disappeared from her face and she laughed nervously. "Does anyone want a snack?" she asked, changing the subject. "I baked some cookies this morning. Cole, have you eaten?"

"Yeah, Sam, uh, Mr. Kerrigan made us some sandwiches," I said, wanting to get away. It creeps me out when Mom talks about the characters on TV as if they're real. "Anyway, I have to call Wayne and tell him I got the job."

I went into the kitchen and dialled. Wayne's mother answered and told me he wasn't home.

"Do you know where he is?"

"He went somewhere with Jack McGraw, but he didn't say where they'd be. Is this Cole?"

"Yeah."

"Well, I'll tell him you called, dear."

"Thanks." I hung up the phone, thought about calling Jack's place in case they were there, and then decided not to bother. I was tired and felt grungy from the day's work. Might as well just shower and go to bed.

Once I was cleaned up, I grabbed a couple of cookies, chased them with a glass of milk, and got ready to turn in. A working man needs his rest.

CHAPTER EIGHT

I ate lunch early on Saturday, stuffed a couple of apples and a bunch of cookies into a bag for an afternoon snack, and headed off to work. I figured I could always scarf down a cookie or two when I was out back, even if Sam didn't give me a break.

As you must know by now, small talk isn't Sam's thing. I didn't even waste my breath saying hello when I got there, just started right in to cleaning. I decided to do the front section, since it would go faster. There are mostly chainsaws, safety pants and boots, and stuff like that there, which was a lot faster to move for scrubbing. I had the whole section done in a couple of hours, and I organized it a bit better when I put things back.

The thing about cleaning is you can really see the dirt other places when you get a spot washed up. Though the area I'd done looked a whole lot better, the grime on the windows behind it was way more noticeable.

"Got any window cleaner?" I asked Sam.

He glanced up from his work, looked first at me then at the windows, shook his head, and went back to what he was doing.

"Well, you need some," I said, surprising myself. "These are filthy."

Sam grunted in a way that could have meant anything.

I shrugged, telling myself if he didn't care about the dirt, I might as well not worry about it either. The strange thing was, it was bothering me. Even though I hadn't exactly made a huge dent in the cleaning, I was feeling proud of the improved appearance of the areas I'd done. I figured that by the end of the next week, I could have the whole place looking pretty decent.

That thought raised a new question in my head. What was Sam going to get me to do once I'd finished washing the shop down? It didn't seem likely that he'd keep me on after that, even though he'd done up a schedule for a month. If he let me go, I'd be right back where I started, with no job and no way to earn money for my Kona.

No sense worrying about it now, I decided. If he didn't keep me on, then he didn't. There was nothing I could do about it.

Jeff Walker came in to pick up his spring around two-thirty, and he seemed surprised to see me there. Actually, most of the customers had looked shocked when they'd seen that Sam had someone working for him.

"Myra told me some young fellow called to say my part was in," Jeff said after I'd gone out back and fetched his spring. "I thought she must be mixed up. Don't remember anyone else ever working here."

"I just started yesterday," I said.

"Well, good for you," Jeff smiled, "good for you. You here for the summer?"

I didn't quite know how to answer that, since Sam was sitting right there within earshot. After realizing earlier that I was soon going to run out of things to do, I was pretty sure the answer was no. Still, I didn't like to say that.

"I guess that depends if Mr. Kerrigan needs me for the whole summer or not," I said.

"Is that so?" Jeff glanced at Sam doubtfully, as if he'd read my mind. "Well, I could use a hand on the farm. If you need work later on, give me a call."

I could hardly believe my ears! There I'd been worrying about my job, and now I had another offer. It would sure be a lot better working for Jeff than for Sam. I nearly told him right then and there that I wanted the job, but it seemed a bit mean to say so in front of Sam.

Instead, I just thanked him and went back to cleaning. *I'll call him tomorrow*, I told myself, *and then I can tell Sam on Monday that I'm quitting*. It would be easier to do on the phone anyway.

By three my stomach was starting to growl. Feeling brave because of the fact that it was going to be my last day, I came right out and asked Sam if I could take a break and have a snack.

The idea of a break seemed foreign to Sam. He looked at me kind of strange, then shrugged. It could have meant anything, but I took it as a yes. I went to the back room, got the cookies and apples out, and took them out front.

"I brought some for both of us," I said, plunking the bag on the counter.

Sam's head came up from the chainsaw he was filing. His eyes settled on me for a long moment, and it was hard to read what was in them.

"My mom made the cookies," I told him. "They're good. Try one."

Sam's big hand reached across the counter and picked up a cookie. He took a bite and chewed it slowly. All the while, he kept looking at me, as if he was puzzled about something. It made me feel weird.

"Good, huh?" I said.

He nodded, still chewing, still staring.

I finished three cookies and an apple, then went back to work, leaving the rest of the food on the counter for Sam. A few minutes later he folded the bag up with what was left and sat it to the side.

"Thanks."

I guess it's normal to say thanks when someone gives you something, but I sure hadn't expected to hear it from Sam. On top of that, his voice sounded kind of strangled, like he had something caught in his throat. It occurred to me then that Sam probably wasn't used to anyone doing nice things for him. It was a safe bet that no one had ever brought him cookies before.

"You're welcome," I said. The funny thing was, my own voice sounded kind of choked up too.

That was the end of our conversation for most the day, but at five-thirty, Sam surprised me for the second time.

"Cole," he said, reaching into the cash register drawer. "Get your window stuff at the hardware store, afore they close."

It was a few seconds before I realized he was sending me for window cleaning supplies, like I'd asked for earlier. Forgetting that I wasn't planning to work for him again after today, I took the money from him and started for the door.

"I'll need one of those squeegee things with a handle, to reach the top," I said. "Is that okay?"

He nodded. "If you need it."

As I walked along the street, I decided that I might just as well keep working for Sam for the next week. Then, when the place was all cleaned, I'd go ahead and take the job with Jeff Walker.

CHAPTER NINE

"Meet me at the bridge in half an hour."

Before I could answer, the line went dead. I'd just finished eating my dinner after work when the phone rang. I'd said hello, then Wayne had blurted that out and hung up.

He does stuff like that, and it usually turns out that he has something cool planned. It's a lot of fun, never knowing what he might be up to next.

I put my dishes in the sink and told Mom I was going out for a while.

"Don't be late," she said automatically, like I might suddenly forget what my curfew is. She reminds me not to be late just about every time I go out in the evening.

"I won't." I headed out the door before she could remind me of any of the other dumb things she likes to tell me, like to be careful for cars and stuff. As if I'm likely to start walking into the street without checking first. Mothers!

Wayne was already at the bridge when I got there. He was standing in the middle, leaning over and looking down at the water, which is hardly more than a wide stream. I saw that he was holding something, but I couldn't make out what it was.

"What's up?" I asked when I reached him.

"I've got a little surprise," he said with a sly smile. He held up a bag and gave it a shake, as though that would tell me what was in it.

"Yeah?" There was something in the way he looked that made me nervous, but that didn't mean anything. Lots of Wayne's ideas make me nervous at first, but we usually pull them off without ending up in trouble. At least, not too much trouble.

There was the time two summers ago that he'd brought a pellet gun to shoot at cars as they went by the old stone hedge out at Riley's Ridge. I'd tried to talk him out of it, but he'd just laughed and called me a girl.

"Nothing will happen," he'd insisted. "It's not like it's a high-powered rifle or anything. We'll just aim for a few tires; it won't even puncture them."

"What if someone has the window down? If we hit the driver by mistake, it could cause an accident," I'd pointed out. Still, I have to admit that part of me had been excited at the idea.

In the end, I'd given in.

We lay on our bellies, hidden in the grass, heads low and hearts pounding from our own daring. Wayne levelled the gun so it was pointed directly at the road, and waited.

A car came by before long and I heard the shot, a sharp click and burst of air as the pellet went whizzing toward its target. We held our breaths listening for the connect sound. There was nothing.

"Darn, missed," Wayne muttered.

He missed the next few shots too, then gave me the gun. My aim was even worse than his, no doubt because my stomach lurched every time I saw a car coming. My finger froze on the trigger, delaying each shot until the car was almost past. Sweat tickled my scalp and neck.

"The tires are too small of a target," Wayne decided, taking the gun back. "I'll wait for some old jalopy, and aim for the fender."

It wasn't long before a beat-up half-ton truck came chugging by, and this time we heard a ping as the pellet slammed into metal.

"Got it!" Wayne whispered, but the triumph faded from his voice as the truck's brake lights came on. "Stay down!" he urged.

The truck was backing up then, and came to a stop almost directly across from us. The driver got out, looked in our direction — though I was pretty sure he couldn't see us — and started to cross the road.

"We've got to get out of here," I whispered. I felt like I might puke. That was when I saw that Wayne was levelling the gun again.

"What are you doing?" I asked, panic rising. With horror, I realized he meant to shoot the driver.

"I'll just hit him in the leg," Wayne hissed. "That'll make him think twice about coming up here."

"No way!" Without thinking, I grabbed the barrel and yanked it down. "I'm getting out of here," I told him, turning and getting into a crouched position, poised for flight.

"Hey! What do you kids think you're doing there?" The man's voice told me he was partway up the hill to our hiding place.

"He saw us." Wayne finally seemed scared too. "We'll have to take off."

We bolted, racing through the grass, and didn't stop until we'd covered the whole length of the field.

"He's not coming," Wayne gasped out after a quick glance behind him. We collapsed into the grass and lay there for a bit. After a while my heart started working normal again.

"That was great," Wayne laughed. "Did you see the look on that guy's face?"

"No." I doubted if he had either. "Who was it anyway?"

"I'm pretty sure it was Gaeton Durelle. He has a green truck like that."

"Think he recognized us?" I felt a shiver run through me. Gaeton wasn't the kind you wanted to cross. He never stood up to anyone face-to-face, but he was known for going overboard when it came to revenge, and it was always something dirty and sneaky that you couldn't pin on him. Once, he'd slashed Buzz Clifford's tires because Buzz had fined him for illegal fishing. Everyone knew it was Gaeton, but it was never proven.

"Naw, adults never know one kid from another," Wayne said.

He'd been all for going back and shooting at some more cars, but I'd had enough. I had been far from convinced that we weren't going to be found out, and it had taken pretty well the whole summer before I could relax about it. It seemed Wayne had been right though, and that Gaeton hadn't recognized who we were.

That was just one of the close calls we've had over the years, so I'd gotten to know that look that Wayne got when he was up to something. And that's the look that was on his face when I arrived at the bridge.

"I liberated this at Jack's place last night," he announced, drawing a bottle out of the bag. It was rum, half full.

"You swiped booze from the McGraws?"

"They have a dozen bottles or more, they'll never miss it." He unscrewed the cap and took a swig, shuddered, then offered it to me.

"I'll be killed if my folks catch me."

"You are *such* a girl." Wayne lurched slightly, and I realized that he'd already been into the rum before I got there. "Anyway, I brought some gum. You can chew it before you get home, to cover up the smell."

I hesitated, then curiosity got the better of me and I took a big swallow. It tasted awful and burned going down. I felt tears in my eyes, and it seemed as though there were some in my throat too.

"This is gross," I said.

"Ain't it though," Wayne agreed cheerfully. He took another drink, shook his shoulders as if that would make it go down quicker, and passed it my way again.

I took another drink, trying to hold my breath so I couldn't taste it this time. It didn't help much. Still, within a few minutes I felt warmth spread all through my body, and a pleasant feeling started to swell up inside me.

"It's not so bad once you get used to it," Wayne observed.

We walked down to the water's edge and sat there taking turns until the bottle was empty. He was right, it went down easier after a few more drinks.

A dragonfly landed nearby and Wayne took a swipe at it, missed, and fell forward. This struck us as hilarious and we laughed until we were out of breath. After that, everything was funny, and I mean everything!

"Hey, the sky is spinning," Wayne slurred, lying back and looking straight up.

I tried it too, and felt dizzy real fast. It was true, everything felt as if it was moving, like the whole world had gone off balance.

Lying there laughing and talking, it was easy to lose track of the time. When I realized that it was already past my curfew, it was with a strange feeling of indifference.

"Gotta go home," I said finally, getting to my feet. I knew I was in trouble when I stood up. What I did after that was probably crazy, though it seemed to make perfect sense at the time.

CHAPTER TEN

Wayne stumbled up the bank behind me and the two of us started unsteadily along the road. Though I confess I had very few of my wits left about me at the time, I did, at least, think going home in that shape was a bad idea. Clearly, we needed to do something to straighten out first.

"Coffee! We gotta get coffee," I said, struck by the brilliance of the notion. In movies, coffee is always a quick and easy solution to help sober people up.

"Yeah, coffee," Wayne nodded solemnly, then went into a fit of laughter.

The immediate problem was where we were going to locate this miracle remedy. The single coffee shop in Kesno is on the other side of town, and my legs were suddenly telling me I had little chance of making it that far. It felt like my knees had become disconnected, and were determined to shoot off in wild directions as I tried to manoeuvre my way along the road.

Going to a friend's house was out of the question too. Anywhere we might go, there would be parents who would be on the phone to our folks in three seconds flat.

I stopped for a moment to consider the problem, though it was difficult to concentrate when my whole body insisted on swaying back and forth. It took several moments before I hit on a solution.

"Sam's!" I said happily. "His house isn' far from 'ere."

"You gotta be kidding."

"No, no, no! Not kidding. It's right on this street." I peered ahead into the darkness. "I think thas it there."

"Thas it there," Wayne mimicked, laughing again.

"He's my employer an' all," I added, seeing that Wayne wasn't convinced of the idea. "I'll just ask him for a cup of coffee. He prolly won't mind. He gave me a sanwish th'other day."

And that's how it happened that, after two days in Sam's employ, I landed on his doorstep late at night and less than sober. I had to knock a few times before he appeared, tucking his shirt into his pants like he'd just got dressed.

"S'cuse me Sam," I offered a smile when he opened the door and peered out into the darkness. "We were wonderin' if you could spare a cuppa coffee."

"Cole?" Sam leaned forward a bit, then stepped backward. He waved a hand in front of his face, coughed a bit, and frowned. "What are you doing here?"

"Lookin' for coffee," I repeated, wondering how he'd missed the first request.

"I see." Sam sighed heavily, frowned some more as if he was thinking hard. Then he stepped back and opened the door. "Come in then. Your friend too."

Wayne and I lurched into the house, which is a small place not much tidier than his shop, although it's cleaner. Sam led us to the kitchen, muttering something I couldn't hear, and told us to sit down.

"You boys are drunk," he said once we'd taken our seats. "Coffee won't change that."

This was highly disappointing news to me, seeing as I'd put all my hopes on getting sobered up real quick.

"Whadya recommend then, Sam?" I asked.

"Not drinking." He shook his head and sighed some more.

"Bit late for that, wha?" Wayne pointed out reasonably. "We gotta, you know, go home soon. Bess not to go like this."

"A shower might help a bit," Sam said doubtfully. "Bathroom's down the hall."

Wayne went first, and he did look somewhat better when he came back to the kitchen. Then it was my turn, and I stood under the streaming water for as long as I could. I felt a bit improved when I was done. On top of that, I felt a great surge of affection for Sam, which was quite a surprise.

"You're a real pal, Sam," I announced when I got back to the kitchen. "Yep, a great guy, that's what you are."

Sam didn't answer. Instead, he gave me a glass of pop, saying something about sugar. I drank it and then he said he was driving us home. I was pretty glad for that, since all I wanted to do by then was crawl into bed and sleep.

We stopped at Wayne's house first, and to my alarm, Sam went to the door with him. I watched as he talked to Wayne's dad for a few minutes, then shuffled back down the walkway and got back in the car.

"My folks will be sleeping by now," I mentioned right off. "No need to come to my door."

He didn't answer, so I figured I'd handled that pretty well. I was wrong. As soon as we got to my place I jumped out of the car and turned to say thanks, which was when I saw that he was out too, and walking toward the door.

"Uh, Sam," I reminded, "You don't need ..."

"It's no trouble," he interrupted. I swear there was a hint of a smile on his face.

I was doomed, and I knew it.

CHAPTER ELEVEN

The door flew open before Sam and I even reached it. Mom and Dad stood there, looking out. They didn't seem happy.

"Cole Fennety! Where on earth have you been?" Mom demanded. "We were worried sick!"

Dad was silent. His eyes travelled back and forth between me and Sam. He took a step forward, his mouth moving as if he was trying to say something and couldn't get the words out.

"What's going on?" Mom just seemed to notice Sam then, and her face got a strange expression on it.

"Boys came to my place," Sam said. "Had a bit of a nip."

"A nip?" Mom's voice got even shriller. "You gave alcohol to teenage boys? What kind of ..."

"'Course not," Sam said. "They came like that."

"We had a shower," I said helpfully. "At Sam's. He drove us home."

"I'm awfully sorry you were put out like this, Sam," Dad said. "We sure appreciate you bringing Cole home."

Sam nodded, shifted from foot to foot. He seemed to be pondering something, then spoke. "Wouldn't like to see the lad in too much trouble. All boys try it sometime."

It took my brain a moment to understand that Sam was taking up for me. I heard Dad say he'd go easy, and that I'd probably learn a lesson from how I felt later anyway.

Sam said he'd be getting back home then. I watched him walk back to his car and drive away. I waved, but he didn't look toward the house.

When I turned around again, Mom and Dad were staring at me. Mom looked like she was going to cry. Her hands were clasped together as if she was wringing something out, though she wasn't holding anything. Dad took a deep breath and started to walk toward me.

All of a sudden it seemed as if they were a long ways away and everything was moving in slow motion. The ground seemed to heave sideways as I took a step forward, and my stomach heaved right along with it.

"I don't feel so good," I said, reaching out for something to hold onto, though there wasn't anything there.

"Imagine that," Dad said, but he put his hand out, steadied me, and led me into the house.

"Get him into the bathroom," Mom said, her voice sharp. It reminded me of the way she talked when we babysat the neighbour's puppy one week. The tone of voice she'd use when she'd tell me to hurry up and take the dog outside before he had yet another accident was the same as she was using then.

I might as well admit that Dad half-carried me down the hallway. We'd hardly reached the toilet when I got sick. Real sick. I thought I was gonna throw up everything I'd ever eaten in my life.

"Ugh," I said when it seemed I was finally through. "That was gross."

"I suppose it was," Dad said. He sounded strangely cheerful.

I thought he was a bit short on sympathy, considering I was suffering plenty. I didn't mention that, though. Instead, I did my best to look pathetic, hoping he'd remember how sick I'd been and go easy on me in the morning.

I didn't expect it was over with by any means. I was sure to get grounded, probably for a couple of years or something, but at the moment, all I really wanted to do was sleep.

Mom came to my room after I'd slid under the covers. She sat there, just looking at me all mournful-like, sighing and shaking her head. She was still there when I fell asleep.

A knock on my door woke me up a little past ten the next morning. I could smell bacon cooking, and I remembered that it was Sunday. My head hurt like you wouldn't believe, as if there was something pounding on the inside, and my mouth was, as Grandpa would say, drier than a burnt boot. A burnt boot might taste better, though.

Thirst won over the urge to lie back down so I got up and went to the kitchen for a glass of water. Mom, Dad, and Jessie were there already, digging into bacon, eggs, toast, and home-fried potatoes. The sight of it made my stomach churn.

"You'd better hurry up and get ready," Mom said, inclining her head toward Jessie with a shake and warning look, as if I needed to be told not to mention anything about the night before in front of her.

"Could I stay home this morning?" I asked. The last thing I felt like doing was going to church.

"No," Dad said quietly. I knew there was no point in arguing.

A shower and a dry slice of toast helped a little, but I still felt pretty rotten as we piled into the car and drove to Gospel House Chapel, where we go every Sunday morning.

I swear that the singing was louder than it had ever been before, and that we got up and down for hymns and prayers and stuff more often than usual. Pastor Stiles must have decided this was the perfect day to go way past the normal closing time too, because he just kept preaching and preaching, while I sat there sweating and feeling as though something was slamming against the inside of my head.

At last it was over. We finally got through the line of people who all stopped to shake the pastor's hand and make some comment about how much they'd enjoyed the service. I could hardly wait to get back home and crash for the rest of the day.

I figured I'd get a lecture first, as soon as one of my folks could do it without Jessie hearing, and find out what kind of consequence I was in for.

"Change your clothes," Dad told me, while Mom put on some soup for lunch. "You and I are going to go to your grandfather's this afternoon."

"Me an' Penelope wanna come too."

"Not this time, Jess." Dad tousled her hair. "You and Mommy can make some girl plans for the day."

Jessie looked like she was going to set up her usual howl, but Mom jumped in and promised that they were going to do something really fun.

A feeling of dread settled on me. Dad was up to something, for sure, and I figured it wasn't going to be good. Surely he wouldn't ask me to split wood, or anything like that, when I felt like I was dying.

"You can tell your grandfather all about last night," he told me once we were on our way.

"But …"

"No buts about it." Dad's jaw was clamped in a firm line. He never said another word the whole way there.

Telling Grandpa what I'd done was the worst possible thing Dad could have come up with. Grandpa is always saying what a great kid I am, how I'm smart and responsible and stuff. I'd rather have been put on bread and water for a year than have to face him and tell him about last night.

That was the first time I really started to think about what had happened, and how I'd gone to Sam's place past midnight, demanding coffee. I could hardly believe I'd done something that stupid, and to Sam, of all people. For sure, that would be the end of my job.

Grandpa's face lit up the minute he saw us.

"Well, well, this is a surprise," he said as he came over and threw an arm around my shoulder.

"Cole wants to take a little walk with you," Dad said, ignoring my pleading look. "He has something he wants to tell you."

Grandpa is no fool. I could tell by the way he glanced at me that he saw there was trouble. He didn't say anything, though, just hauled on his boots while Dad went in to talk to Aunt Betty, and we headed out.

For the first ten minutes or so, we just walked in silence. Every time I tried to get words out, they got stuck in my throat. Then we reached a place where there were some tree stumps from where he'd harvested some wood. Grandpa stopped, sat down on one, and indicated with a nod that I was to do the same.

"I been around a fair number of years," he said solemnly, "so I don't think what you have to say is going to come as much of a shock. You want to go ahead and tell me?"

"I did something pretty dumb." I swallowed, wishing we'd brought a canteen of water.

"I don't suppose you're the first to get in this kind of racket."

I looked at him, surprised. It seemed as if he already knew the whole story.

"Oh, I recognize a hangover when I see it." He smiled, reading my expression. "Appears you had yourself a little drink last night."

He didn't look upset or anything, which made it a lot easier to tell him the whole story. The only time his eyebrows raised a bit was when I got the part about how we'd gone to Sam's place.

"Well, if that don't beat all," he said, when I told him how Sam drove us home. "Sam Kerrigan, no less. And you say you've been working for him?"

"I was," I said miserably. "I don't suppose I am anymore. Not after that."

CHAPTER TWELVE

Grandpa didn't lecture me or anything. He didn't even seem all that shocked or upset, the way I'd expected.

"I guess most young fellers around your age are going to try a drink," he said quietly, once I'd finished telling him the whole story. "That don't make it right, or good, but it's a fact all right. The thing is, a person has to make a lot of decisions in life, and you've come to a place where you have to make a big one.

"In my experience, liquor causes a whole lot of trouble for a whole lot of people. I personally ain't never seen any good come from drinkin'. But you got to make up your mind whether it's something you want to do again or not."

"Never!" I said, and meant it too.

"It's easy to say that when you're feelin' as you are

right now, Cole. There's goin' to be other times though, when you're in situations that will tempt you. Best idea is to make your mind up solid, so when those times come, you have your answer ready.

"I ain't much of a churchgoer, as you know. But I do read the Good Book and say a little prayer now and then. There's a story in there that comes to mind, about Daniel. You know all about him an' the lion's den, I reckon."

"Yeah."

"Well, there's something else in there that might not seem as big a thing as being thrown in with a bunch of lions, but it's worth thinkin' on."

Grandpa paused and took a deep breath. "I ain't aimin' to get all preachy on you, Cole. Never does much good, tellin' a person what to do. But in this story, Daniel and a bunch of others were captured and taken to live in King Nebuchadnezzar's court. And they were expected to eat stuff they weren't supposed to eat, you know, according to their religion.

"Now, here's the part I like. It says, in the Good Book, that Daniel *purposed in his heart* that he would not defile himself by eating that food and going against what he believed was right. He didn't either, and he got stronger and healthier than the others."

I didn't quite see what that had to do with drinking, but I nodded anyway, to show Grandpa that I'd been listening.

"You see, Cole, in that story, Daniel already had his mind made up. He didn't sit down to a big table loaded with food when he was hungry, and decide then, when it would have been mighty tempting to dig in. No sir, he already knew what he was going to do beforehand, 'cause he'd, as it says, purposed in his heart ahead of time. That's what I like. He'd picked right over wrong *before* he got in a spot where he might have made a different choice."

I saw what he was getting at then.

"So, you think on it, and make your mind up solid, Cole. Then when the time comes, you'll be ready." Grandpa stood, stretched a bit, and inclined his head in the direction of the house. "We best be gettin' back now. You look like you could use a bit of a rest."

Back at the house, Dad was in the kitchen, having a cup of tea with Aunt Betty. When we went in, he glanced back and forth between me and Grandpa, and seemed satisfied with what he saw.

We stayed for a little while longer, and Aunt Betty fussed over me the way she always does, trying to get me to eat "a little something", which is how she refers to the mountains of food she piles on the table, like I'm liable to starve if she doesn't stuff me full of food every time she sees me.

Mom and Jessie were busy making play dough when we got back home, and from what I could gather they were on their second batch. There were already three lumps of it on the table, coloured yellow, green, and blue. Apparently, Jessie *needed* red and they'd forgotten to make that colour the first time.

First chance she got, Mom took me aside. "Cole," she said, "I think maybe you should call Mr. Kerrigan and apologize for the trouble you put him to last night."

When Mom says she "thinks maybe" I should do something she's not making a suggestion — she's giving an order.

"I don't know if he has a phone," I said lamely. She frowned and put her hands on her hips, like I'd said something real saucy or rude.

"I'll look in the phone book." I sighed, got it, found the number, and started to dial. Meanwhile, Mom stood there watching and waiting.

"I'd rather do this privately," I said. She folded her hands across her waist and stayed put.

"Yeah?" Sam answered on the fourth ring, just when I was getting all hopeful that he wasn't there.

"Sa ... uh, Mr. Kerrigan, this is Cole."

Silence.

"I'm calling to apologize for last night, sir. I'm real sorry for going to your place like that, and for putting you to all that trouble and all."

Silence.

"And, uh, I also wanted to thank you for helping me and my friend out the way you did." I felt sweat forming on my forehead and wasn't sure if it was nervousness or part of the after-effects from the night before.

"Well, I guess that's all then." I cast about for some way to close the conversation, seeing as how there was nothing being said on the other end of the line. "Except that it will never happen again, and I'm, as I said, really, really sorry."

Then the weirdest thing happened. Sam started chuckling. I stood there, holding the phone, half in shock, while he progressed to outright laughter.

"Call me Sam," he said when he finally spoke.

"Yes, sir, uh, Sam." I didn't know what to make of his amusement.

"I'll see you at work," he said then, and hung up.

It seemed I'd gotten off pretty easy for the whole mess, what with Grandpa's and Sam's reactions being a lot different than I'd expected. I even still had my job.

I should have known that wasn't the end of it where Mom and Dad were concerned. Later that night, after Jessie had gone to bed (complaining, as usual, that it's *not fair* she has to go to bed before anyone else, as if she's not enough of a tyrant when she gets her proper rest — I can't even imagine what she'd be like if she was tired and cranky!) they sat me down for A Talk.

What A Talk means, in our house, is a lecture followed by a punishment, only they call it a consequence. They took turns pointing out all the stuff I already knew from the experience, like how drinking makes a person do dumb things, and how it isn't much fun to be sick afterward. I just listened, wanting them to get to the "consequence" part so it could be over and done and I could go to bed. I still felt kind of like I'd been hit by a truck.

"Obviously, with a job, you can't be grounded completely," Dad said at last. "But aside from going to work, you won't leave this house for the next two weeks."

"And I don't think you should be hanging around with Wayne anymore," Mom added. "He's not a good influence, though of course, you're responsible for your own actions."

"But Wayne is my best friend," I protested. I looked at Dad to see if he was going to say anything to help change Mom's mind, but he just stared right through me.

It wasn't fair! I knew I deserved to be punished, but that was too much.

I went off to bed without another word, though. I'd have to figure something out later.

CHAPTER THIRTEEN

"**M**ornin'."

I stopped dead in my tracks, half convinced I'd imagined the greeting. Sam was in his usual place at the counter, sharpening a long blade from some kind of farm machine. He hadn't looked up or anything as I was walking past to take my lunch to the back room, and the single word startled me. He didn't even sound quite as gruff as usual.

"Morning, Sam," I said as nonchalant as I could, as if it was a regular thing for him to say hello like any normal human being. Realizing I was standing there gawking like an idiot, I hurried to put my bag of food away and get to work.

The first thing I wanted to do that morning was get at the windows. On Saturday, when I'd gone to the store to buy supplies, Mrs. Peterson had been on the cash.

"You aiming to use this here window cleaner with the squeegee?" she'd asked me as she started to ring in my purchases.

"Yes'm."

"Nope." She put it to the side. "You'll be using a bucket, right?"

I nodded.

"Well, this stuff is okay for spraying on and wiping down with paper towels, but if you're using a bucket of water, you'll want to put vinegar and soda in it, not this. It's cheaper and it works better."

She'd sent me back to get a jug of vinegar and a box of baking soda, then explained how to mix it. I guess she didn't trust my memory, 'cause even after she'd gone over it twice, she stopped and wrote it down on a piece of paper.

I measured the water, soda, and vinegar according to her instructions and lugged the bucket out to the front room. The squeegee had a handle that you could adjust for length, and I pulled it out as long as it would go and locked it in place.

There's a guy who does most of the store windows in town and I'd seen him at it lots of times. Looked like there was nothing to it — just apply the cleaner and then scrape it dry with the rubber blade. Only it wasn't that easy at all. I couldn't seem to get the hang of the way I'd seen him do it, making side-to-side sweeps with the rubber edge, and there were streaks and smudges all over the place when I'd finished the first big window.

Deciding I must need fresh water, I moved on and did the insides of all four large windows, then went and changed the water. I did them over. By then, I was getting better at using the squeegee and I'd also remembered that the town's window cleaner always had a rag in his hand and wiped the rubber blade down between passes. That made a big difference.

The outsides were next and I repeated the whole process. There was a huge improvement, but I wasn't entirely satisfied. There seemed to be a thin film remaining, even after being washed twice, inside and out. I did them a third time and stood back, checking from different angles to make sure the final coat of grime had come off.

They looked good. Next, I washed down the ledges and frames, which also needed more than one cleaning before all the dirt was gone.

It was a slow morning for customers, but the few who came in commented on the improvements all my scrubbing was making in the place.

Sam was finished with his blade long before I finished with the windows. I was surprised to see that he was just sitting there, doing nothing.

"Need me to get anything for you?" I asked as I went by.

"Just takin' a little rest," he said, shaking his head. His voice sounded strained.

I looked at him close then and saw that he was almost wincing.

"Something wrong, Sam?"

He didn't answer. Instead, he went and fetched a chainsaw, hoisted it onto the counter, and started to take it apart.

I shrugged and went back to work. We stopped at lunchtime and ate. Sam had his usual bologna sandwiches; I had a chicken and cold salad plate Mom had made up out of leftovers from our dinner the night before. When she'd passed it to me in the morning, I'd known she was softening up a bit, which raised my hopes that I could persuade her on the subject of Wayne pretty soon.

"Mom sent cake for both of us," I said, opening the square plastic container she'd packed two generous pieces in. Sam looked at it the same way he'd stared at me the day I'd shared cookies with him.

"Later," he said. He reached into his pocket and took out a small tin can, opened it, and lifted out a couple of pills.

"Headache," he explained.

"If you're not feeling good, maybe you should lay down out back for a bit," I suggested, sympathetic because of how rotten I'd felt the day before. "I can take care of customers if you show me how to work the cash register."

He seemed to weigh the idea, but then shook his head. "Just a headache," he said.

Probably doesn't trust me, I thought, angry at the idea. *Well, he can work with his head aching for all I care.*

"Afternoon, Sam."

I looked over to see that Buddy Anderson had come in. He had on safety pants, the kind that loggers use to protect their legs while they're falling trees. Buddy's not a logger, though, which is why his pants were in good shape, not all torn and scruffy the way they get in no time if you're working in the woods regular. They rose from the top of bright orange boots, which looked like ordinary rubber boots but I knew had steel toes in them.

"Thought I'd clear a few of those darned poplars off the back of my property," he said, lifting his saw, a big Husky, onto the counter. "Too darned dull, though. I could take down trees with my teeth easier. Can you give it a little rub?"

Sam pointed to the counter and picked up a file. He looked kind of disgusted, and I was pretty sure I knew why. Grandpa says a man who can't file his own saw oughtn't even own one.

"Some fellers just buy a saw fer the sake of havin' it," he said, "like it makes 'em more manly or sumthin'.

Don't look too manly, though, havin' to ask another man to put an edge on it."

Sam's fingers flew as he sharpened the Husqvarna, moving with the ease and skill of someone who's had countless hours of practice. I sure wished I could learn to do it that fast, but the times Grandpa had let me work on his, my movements were slow and clumsy. He'd said I had the right stroke though, and would get good at it in time.

"Five dollars, right?" Buddy asked, reaching for his wallet when Sam was done.

"Ring that in, Cole," Sam said to me.

I took the bill and went to the cash register, a big old-fashioned kind, not like the ones that scan bar codes. Sam told me what keys to hit, and the door flew open when I'd done what he said. I stuck the money in with the other fives and slammed it shut, feeling strangely proud.

CHAPTER FOURTEEN

Being grounded and all, I really looked forward to going to work. At least it got me out of the house and away from Jessie, who seemed to be getting even more aggravating all the time, though I hadn't thought that was possible.

The dumb doll that she carried around everywhere she went had become another huge source of annoyance. I guess this sounds kind of stupid, but I'd come to hate that doll. The sight of it, hanging limply as she dragged it about, was really getting on my nerves.

Jessie was worse than Mom, going on about Penelope as if it was real, like Mom does about her soap operas sometimes. Hearing her constant claims that "Penelope wants this" and "Penelope wants that" was driving me half crazy. And, of course, the regular complaints that I'd been *mean* to her and Penelope weren't helping.

I decided it was time to do something about it. *She's gotta put it down sometime*, I told myself, and started watching for an opportunity. I also had to figure out a way to get rid of it without getting caught, which was going to be the tricky part.

On Thursday evening, I saw the perfect chance. Cassie, a girl from down the road, was over, which doesn't happen all that often. Jessie is so bossy that not too many kids come around, and when they do, they generally don't stay for long.

Well, Cassie had been going down the street pushing this big old-fashioned-looking carriage with some of her dolls in it. Jessie spied her as she ambled past and ran out to the front yard.

"Hi, Cassie," she said, putting on her phoney, friendly voice. "Wanna come in an' play with me an' Penelope?"

Cassie looked doubtful, but she also looked bored. I guess she decided that even playing with Jessie was better than just ambling up and down the street, since she turned the bulky carriage around and came up our walk.

In no time, they had an assortment of dolls all sitting around the yard, propped up and looking ridiculous in their frilly little dresses. That gave me an idea, though.

"You girls should dress up to look like the dolls' mothers," I suggested in an offhand way. Jessie has a trunk full of old clothes for dressing up like that, long skirts and puffy blouses and stuff.

The idea appealed to them, just like I knew it would. They ran off into the house to change, leaving the collection of dolls outside. The second they were out of sight, I grabbed Penelope and stuffed her into the carriage, underneath the folded blanket that was in it. I laid her out flat, so the extra bulge was hardly noticeable.

It worked out even better than I'd planned, because a few minutes later, Cassie came storming out of the house. I gathered, from the angry remarks flying between the two girls, that there had been an argument about who got to wear what. Naturally, Jessie couldn't be gracious and let her guest pick an outfit she liked. Oh, no, not Jessie.

So, there was Cassie, in a snit, flying around the yard picking up her dolls and putting them back in the carriage while Jessie alternated between pouting and complaining loudly that they were *her* clothes so *she* should get to decide who wore what.

Cassie was having none of it. She finished gathering up her dolls and stomped off, pushing along the carriage that, unknown to her, contained the dreaded Penelope.

I watched her walk out of sight, then ambled back into the house and waited for the howl that I knew was coming. It didn't take long. Jessie noticed that Penelope wasn't there as soon as she started to pick up her dolls. She flew into the house, screeching at the top of her lungs.

"Jessie, calm down!" Mom said. "What on earth is the matter?"

Between sobs and shrieks, Jessie informed us that Penelope had been kidnapped.

"Are you sure she was outside?" I asked innocently. "Maybe you brought her in the house when you came in to change."

"I *didn't*," she insisted, but she went to look around anyway.

She searched high and low and (I swear this is true) she kept calling the stupid thing's name. What did she think: it was going to answer her? What a moron!

After searching through the house, she went back outside and checked the yard again. I watched through the window. Tears were running down her face the whole time, and I could see her shoulders shaking. I had to remind myself that she'd been torturing me with the dumb doll for months.

Suddenly, the door banged open and she stomped into the house.

"Cassie stole her!" she announced. That's just like Jessie. As soon as an idea pops into her head, she decides it's got to be the truth.

"Now, Jessie," Mom said, "it's not nice to make accusations like that. I'm sure that if Cassie took it, it was a mistake. Why don't you call and ask if she picked up Penelope by accident?"

Jessie called and asked, though I must say her tone of voice was pretty hostile and accusing. I held my breath while Jessie waited for Cassie to go check the carriage to see if Penelope was in it.

"She *says* Penelope isn't there," Jessie said, hanging up the phone a moment later, "but I *know* she has her."

Mom tried to persuade her that it was wrong to talk that way, like Jessie ever listened to reason. I felt a bit weird about it, since I knew Cassie *did* have the doll.

I had a moment of anxiety when Jessie said she was going over there to find Penelope. I could just picture her ripping that carriage apart and finding it in the bottom. I told myself that the worst-case scenario would be that I'd have to put up with it again. Cassie would get the blame — there'd be no reason for anyone to suspect I'd had anything to do with it. But Mom wouldn't let her go over to Cassie's place. Mom said that, most likely, some dog had picked in up and carried it off.

Jessie spent the next few days moping around, whining about Penelope's disappearance. You'd think I would have enjoyed that, considering how much she'd pestered me with it, but it wasn't quite like that. The way she kind of deflated and went around with a long, sad face was kind of pathetic.

It made me start thinking about how that doll was the closest thing Jessie had to a friend.

CHAPTER FIFTEEN

I hadn't seen or talked to Wayne since the night we'd gotten in trouble, and I'd figured he wasn't allowed out or anything either. Then, on my way to work the next Saturday, I saw him leaning against the hydro pole at the corner of Water Street.

"What's with your mother?" he asked, without even saying hello first. "Is she, like, psycho or what?"

"What do you mean?"

"I called you a few days ago and she told me never to phone there again. What's her problem?"

I told him about getting grounded and how my folks had said I couldn't hang out with him anymore.

"That's retarded," he said. "What'd you tell them?"

"I didn't really say much about it yet." I felt stupid admitting this, because I knew if Wayne's parents tried something like that with him, he'd find a way around it in no time. "I was kind of waiting for them to cool down before I brought it up."

Wayne shook his head. "You can't let them get away with stuff like that," he said, as if it was up to me. "You gotta stand up for yourself."

"Your folks didn't wig out or anything?" I asked, hoping to steer the subject in a new direction.

"Heck no." He smirked. "Well, they tried, at first. I straightened them out quick enough."

"How do you mean?"

"Oh, they were going on about it, you know, the usual raving. I just told them I hadn't known what was in the bottle. Looked innocent and hurt that they didn't trust me." He paused to laugh. "Then, just when they'd bought that, Jack's old man called and said I stole the rum from his place."

"What did you do?" I remembered Wayne insisting that Mr. McGraw would never miss it.

"I yelled at them."

"You *yelled* at them?" I didn't see how that would have helped.

"Yeah, like, how could you believe that I'd do something like that? Jack *gave* it to me, and now he's trying to save his own neck by acting like I took it.

"Then they asked me, hadn't Jack told me what it was when he gave it to me? So, I says, not really. He said it was something his dad made himself and just put in an old liquor bottle. Some kind of homemade berry drink."

"And they *believed* that?"

"Sure they did. They even apologized for not trusting me." Wayne put his head back and laughed. "Man, they're so totally gullible."

I'd have picked a different word to describe parents who'd fall for a story like that, but I didn't say that to him. He sure knows how to handle his folks. I wish I could get away with half the things he does.

"I can't wait to get my hands on some more of that stuff," he went on. "It was great, wasn't it?"

"Yeah, great." I tried to sound enthusiastic, but it was hard when all I could picture was leaning over the flush, retching my guts out.

"I think I might be able to get something tonight," he went on. "That geeky Lisa Manderson called me again today. She just never gets the hint, calls me every month or so, like I might suddenly find her more appealing than a pig's arse. I was going to tell her to go play with her acne kit until I remembered that her dad is a bigwig and her folks do a lot of entertaining. Bound to be a lot of booze floating around their place."

I assumed he was about to tell me he was going to swipe a bottle from the Mandersons', but I was wrong.

"I told her to meet me here. In fact, the bowser should be along any minute. Hope I can stay focused on the mission long enough to put up with her ugly puss."

"She's bringing you a bottle?" I know Lisa pretty well, since she's been in our classes since first grade, and I couldn't quite picture her stealing from her own folks. She's also not nearly as bad as Wayne was making her out to be, though you couldn't exactly call her pretty.

"Nah, I'm not stupid. She'd be suspicious if I asked her to do that right off. I have to persuade her that I like her, and that I want to party with her tonight. I'll get her to bring me something this evening."

"You're going to drink with her?"

"For a little while, just to keep her cooperative for another time. I'll think of some reason I have to leave early, and meet you later on."

"I'm grounded," I reminded him.

"So, say you're sick and go to bed early, then sneak out the window."

"Won't work. My mom always checks on me when I'm in bed sick."

"Then tell them you have to work late. Inventory or something." Wayne was getting impatient. "Can't you think of anything on your own?"

"They might check. Anyway, I'd get caught when I went home. They'd smell it."

"You are *such* a girl sometimes, Cole. Maybe you should borrow some of your mommy's skirts."

"Knock it off, Wayne. You know my folks are a lot stricter than yours."

"Knock it off, Wayne," he mimicked in a falsetto voice. "You know my folks are a lot stricter than yours."

"You want to know the truth?" I was angry by then. "I got sick as a dog last Saturday, and I'm not interested in drinking again."

"Oh, for —" Wayne broke off, smiled wide, and said, "Well, *hello* there."

The sudden change startled me until I realized Lisa was coming along the sidewalk behind me. She had her hair fixed up, and was wearing lipstick and stuff.

"Hi, Wayne," she smiled back shyly. "Hi, Cole."

"Hi, Lisa."

"Wow, you sure look good today." Wayne looked her up and down. She blushed and lowered her eyes.

"Cole here is just on his way to work," Wayne said, slipping an arm around her back. "What say you and I take a little walk? Find ourselves some nice quiet place."

Lisa giggled and looked up at Wayne adoringly. She's had a crush on him forever, and her happiness was just shining all over the place.

It made me sick.

CHAPTER SIXTEEN

It was hard to concentrate at work that afternoon. I kept thinking about Lisa and how bad she was going to feel when she realized Wayne was just using her. Besides, she was bound to get in a lot of trouble at home if she got caught stealing and drinking. From what I've heard about her father, Ted Manderson, he's not the nicest person in Kesno. There have even been rumours about him hitting his wife and kids sometimes, though not every story that gets told around here is true.

The thing that bothered me the most was that I knew Wayne wouldn't care. Whatever happened to her, he'd just laugh it off. There have been lots of times I've wished I could be more like that, instead of letting things get to me. This time, though, I was really disgusted with him.

I was turning all this over in my head, and not paying very close attention to what I was doing, when I realized

Sam was bent over the counter. Well, Sam is always bent over the counter, but there was something different in his posture this time. I went to his side, casual-like, so I could see what was up.

As soon as I got close to him, I could see that there were beads of sweat on his forehead, and his face was twisted up in a weird way.

"Sam?" I leaned down. "What is it?"

"Just one of my headaches," he said in a sort of gasp. "Bad one."

As he spoke, he gripped the edge of the counter, like he might fall over. I took his arm automatically, to help steady him.

"Come on," I said firmly, "you're going to lie down out back."

Instead of the argument I expected, Sam nodded and let me help him out to the couch in the other room.

"Do you have your pills with you?" I asked, remembering he'd taken some the last time he'd had a headache. He patted his shirt pocket, face ashen, and grimaced.

"Left 'em home."

"Want me to go to your place and get them? It will only take a few minutes."

He fumbled in his pants' pocket and brought out a set of keys. "Kitchen table," he groaned, passing me the keys.

I took the keys, then remembered that when any of us have a headache at home, Mom always puts a cold, wet cloth on our foreheads. I found a small towel in the bathroom cabinet, ran cold water on it, wrung it out, and folded it into a rectangle.

"This might help till I get back," I said, laying it over his brow. "I'll be quick."

I ran all the way to Sam's place and let myself in. Just as he'd said, there was a pill bottle on the kitchen table. I snatched it up and hurried back to the shop.

When I got there with the pills, I found Sam lying with his knees drawn up, sort of rocking himself. I filled a glass with water and kneeled down beside him.

"Here you go, Sam." I opened the pill bottle and passed it to him.

He shook a couple of pills into his palm, tossed them into his mouth, and took a big gulp of water to wash them down. Then he laid back on the couch again and closed his eyes.

"Thanks, Cole."

"Yeah, no problem, Sam. I, uh, hope you feel better soon." I stood and watched him for a few seconds before going back out front. His face had a kind of grey pallor to it. I figured the headaches he got must be migraines. My friend James Chevarie's mom gets those and she has special pills for them too. I went there one time when she was sick and he said she couldn't stand the slightest amount of noise, or even having the light on, when she got a migraine, so we couldn't stay in the house.

I went and turned off the light in the back room, and did my best to be real quiet until Sam got back up a half-hour later.

"Is your headache gone?" I was a bit surprised, since James had told me that his mom would be in bed for hours. Maybe Sam's pills worked better than hers.

"Pretty much," he said, going to his usual place at the counter and starting his tinkering. "Ray Mutch needs this pump fixed today. He's coming in for it before closing."

The rest of the day flew past with a lot of customers in and out. I was taking care of the cash register most of the time by then, and no longer needed Sam to tell me how to ring in purchases. Ray got there just before six.

"Were you able to save it?" he asked, seeing his pump on the counter.

"Just needed a bearing," Sam said.

"Great!" Ray said. "I thought for sure it was a goner. Darned thing was scaring the cows, the way it was grinding and screeching. So, what do I owe you?"

"Sixty-five."

"Man, that beats buying a new one." Ray looked pleased as he counted out the money. "This model is over three hundred bucks. Can't do without it though, with a herd that size to keep watered."

As we locked up, I remembered that I'd been planning to quit and go work for Jeff Walker at the end of the week. I was getting new responsibilities at Sam's all the time, though, and what with his headaches and all, it seemed wrong to up and leave. I made my mind up right then and there that I'd stay for the summer if he wanted me. Besides, he was acting more and more human all the time.

As we stepped out on the sidewalk, Sam passed me an envelope and told me it was my pay. I stuffed it in my pocket, even though I was anxious to see how much was in it.

We walked along Water Street together, but when we came to the place where I'd normally turn toward my place, I noticed Sam looked kind of poorly again. Without saying anything about it, I just kept on with him until we got to his house.

"Should I expect you later tonight?" he asked as he unlocked his door. His voice was gruff, but there was a trace of a smile on his mouth.

"No, I don't think so." I felt a bit foolish, thinking of the way I'd barged in on him the Saturday before.

"I'll see you next week then." He reached out his hand and gave me a tap on the shoulder before going into his house. I swear he was grinning!

When I got home, I hauled the envelope out of my pocket and counted the bills in it. I had to count them twice before I actually believed how much was there. Sam was paying me eight dollars an hour — almost two dollars more than minimum wage!

CHAPTER SEVENTEEN

After lunch on Sunday, we were all getting ready to go to Grandpa's place when the phone rang. Mom answered it.

"Cole, it's for you," she called. "It's a *girl*."

Even though she put her hand over the mouthpiece to announce this, I wasn't what you'd call pleased. I don't get a lot of calls from girls (not that I want them pestering me or anything) and the last thing I needed was for Mom to make a big production of it.

I took the phone from her and gave her a look that meant a little privacy would be nice. Amazingly, she took the hint and left the room, though not before raising her eyebrows and giving me a weird smile.

"Hello," I said, making sure I kept my voice low. Sometimes it goes all high and squeaky, which is pretty embarrassing.

"Hey, dude!"

"Wayne?" I whispered in surprise.

"Yeah." He laughed. "I got my sister to ask for you. Smart, huh?"

"I guess."

"Now I can call anytime I want and your crazy mother won't even know."

"Uh-huh. What's up?" I didn't exactly appreciate him calling my mom crazy, but I let it go.

"You didn't show up last night," he said.

"I told you I couldn't."

"Yeah, I know. I just thought you might change your mind."

"So, did Lisa make it?" I changed the subject.

"Oh, *yeah*. Brought a bottle of vodka too." His voice was smug. "Man, that chick would do anything I asked her to."

"Well, good for you." I couldn't hide the fact that I didn't think much of the whole thing.

"She's *real* friendly," he continued, ignoring my tone of voice. "If I hadn't been so anxious to get rid of her, I could have ..."

"I gotta go," I cut him off. "We're heading out to my grandfather's place."

"Well, *excuse* me," he said. "Can you get out of the house tomorrow?"

"No, Wayne, I can't. I'm still grounded, except

for work, remember?"

"Yeah, yeah." His voice dropped then. "Look, Cole, try to talk to your folks, okay? I mean, you're my best friend, man. It's weird, not being able to hang out."

"I will," I promised. "See ya."

I'd barely put the phone down when Mom came back into the room. She was smiling and giving me questioning looks. I pretended not to notice.

"Well?" she said after a series of strange faces failed to get a response.

"Well what?"

"Who was that?"

"Just a friend," I said vaguely.

"And does this friend have a name?"

"Nope. Some parents don't bother naming their kids."

"Don't be smart, young man."

"Well, do I have to be interrogated every time someone phones me?"

Just then, Dad stuck his head in the doorway and said it was time to go. I'm pretty sure he heard what was going on and was rescuing me. We piled into the car and headed out to Grandpa's place.

Normally, Jessie is a total nuisance when we're in the car, but not this time. She just sat there, staring out the window and not saying a thing. After a minute or two of this, I realized she was peering around the way you do when you're looking for something specific. It didn't take much brainpower to figure out what it was.

She'd been so woebegone since that stupid doll disappeared, it was like having a completely different sister. Instead of driving me crazy, she just moped around all forlorn. I guess I should have been happy that she wasn't annoying me full-time anymore.

"Wanna count cars?" I asked. That was a game she sometimes pestered me to play. We'd each pick a colour and see how many each of us saw by the time we got where we were going. It was pretty boring, and I usually only went along with it if she whined until Mom made me.

Jessie just shook her head and kept gawking out the window. I saw that she was biting her bottom lip, like she was trying not to cry. By the time we reached the edge of town she stopped looking and put her head down.

She'll get over it, I told myself. The next thing, I saw a tear run down her cheek. She lifted her hand and wiped it away, then turned and glared at me.

"Leave me alone," she said, as though I'd been bothering her. I guess she didn't want anyone looking at her.

"Now, Jessie, don't be like that. Cole isn't doing anything to you, and it's not his fault your doll is gone," Mom said. "Why, just a moment ago he was trying to cheer you up by offering to play a game with you."

Mom gave me an approving look to let me know how nice that had been of me. I felt like a total jerk.

When we got to Grandpa's, all I wanted was to get away from Jessie and her sad face. As soon as I could, I asked Dad if I could go over to Jeff Walker's place for a while. He must have forgotten I was grounded, because he said yes.

I walked along the road, trying to enjoy my temporary freedom on a warm summer day, but it was pretty hard with the picture in my head of Jessie crying. Of course, she's always going on about something, but this was different.

The Walkers' truck wasn't in the yard when I got there, and I was about to turn around and go back to Grandpa's when I heard someone call my name. I looked around but couldn't see anyone.

"I saw you coming down the road. Looked like you just lost your best friend."

I recognized the voice as Rhonda's, but there was no sign of her.

"Up here," she called. "In the tree."

"Oh." I saw her then, sitting perched in a big maple off to the left side of their yard. "What are you doing up there?"

"I got chased up by a pack of wolves."

"Wolves? Really?" I looked around nervously but didn't see anything. "When?"

"A few minutes ago. They can't have gone far, so be careful." Rhonda peered about and then pointed. "I think I see a couple of them coming back. You'd better come up."

Without hesitating, I scrambled up the tree and edged out on the big limb where she was sitting. She moved over a bit to make room for me.

"Where are your folks?" I asked, wondering how long we might be stuck up there.

"Gone to Elmer's place up the road. Won't be home till suppertime." She didn't seem too concerned.

"I didn't think wolves bothered people."

"Not usually. They must have rabies or something. I think a few of them were, you know, frothing at the mouth."

I still hadn't got so much as a glimpse of one of them, but I wasn't going to argue with her. I wasn't about to take any chances with a pack of rabid wolves.

"So, you guys visiting at your grandfather's place?"

"Yeah." I wished I'd stayed there, but didn't say so in case Rhonda thought I was cowardly or something.

We spent the next fifteen or twenty minutes just sitting there, talking and keeping an eye out for any sign that the wolves were still around. Then, all of a sudden, Rhonda swung her legs over, held onto the limb for a second or two, and then dropped to the ground. I was too astonished to speak.

"You hungry?" she asked, turning her face up to where I was still sitting. "There's some chocolate layer cake in the kitchen."

"But the wolves," I protested. It was a few hundred yards to the side of the house. I could just imagine the pack there, lying low, waiting, their eyes mad and foam dripping from their tongues. "You'd better get back up here."

"Nah, they're gone now," she said causally as she sauntered toward the house. "Come on."

The chilling picture that had formed in my mind of her being torn to shreds by the crazed wolves disappeared in a flash as I realized that she'd been having me on.

"You tricked me," I accused, climbing down and running after her.

"Yeah," she laughed. "It was easy, too."

"Why'd you do it?"

"Just for fun. I like to pretend stuff like that sometimes." She was opening the back door of the house then. "Mom puts pudding in the middle of her chocolate cake. You want milk or pop with yours?"

"Milk," I mumbled. I told myself I should just leave, but my feet kept on into the kitchen. I told myself it was only because the cake sounded so good.

CHAPTER EIGHTEEN

"I hear you're working for old Sam Kerrigan," Rhonda commented as she sat a huge slab of cake in front of me.

"Yeah," I said as I picked up the fork and stabbed, bringing a big bite up to my mouth. It was delicious all right. I noticed that the piece of cake she took was just as big as mine. Usually girls go on about their figures and stuff and hardly eat at all, or at least, they act like they don't.

"Does he whip you to make you work harder?"

"Yup. Gives me ten lashes every morning," I said.

"Well, I'm sure you deserve it." She smiled. There was a small blob of icing on her lip and she must have realized it because she dabbed it with a napkin. It was kind of cute, the way she did that instead of just licking it off.

"Actually, Sam's a pretty good guy to work for after all," I told her before shovelling more cake in. "He doesn't talk a whole lot, but he's not mean the way people think."

"He could have been your grandfather, you know. If things had turned out different, that is."

I looked up in surprise and asked what she meant by that.

"He used to go out with your grandmother, back when they were young."

"Where'd you hear that?"

"My great-aunt Ruby told me. Said they used to step out together and that they'd been quite an item at one time. That's the way they described dating back then. Anyway, Sam had to go away for a while and she up and married your grandfather while he was gone."

The idea of Sam dating anyone was really weird. That it had been my grandmother was even odder.

"Aunt Ruby said that Sam never got over it, and never looked at another woman after that."

I figured that was just dumb romance talk, which females are so fond of, but it was still strange to think about. I just kept eating my cake and didn't say anything else about it, hoping she wouldn't either. The last thing a guy wants to hear is a bunch of mush.

Rhonda must have taken the hint because she dropped the subject. We ate in silence until our cake was gone.

"Want another piece?"

"No, I'm stuffed. That was great, though, thanks."

"Wanna come with me and give Century and Whisper some sugar cubes?"

"Sure," I agreed. We headed out to the field where the horses were.

"Better approach them slowly," she cautioned, "they might be nervous."

"How come?"

"You know, after that pack of rabid wolves was around." Rhonda stole a quick glance at me and then giggled.

I felt my face getting hot and hoped I wasn't turning red.

"I'll get you back for that," I promised.

"You were up that tree like a bolt of lightning!" She laughed outright then, laughed until she started staggering and gasping for breath. I watched in annoyance as she tried to get herself under control.

"I wish I'd had a camera," she said, struggling for breath. Then she lurched sideways, overcome with amusement (at *my* expense!), and collided with me.

I caught her automatically, to keep her from falling, though it would have served her right. She put a hand on my chest to steady herself.

"I was just having fun," she said, her laughter fading. "Sorry."

I didn't think she was the least bit sorry, but my anger was moving off fast. She was so close, looking at me — right at me — and there was just the slightest trace of a smile left on her face. Only this smile was different, kind of questioning or something.

I realized I was still holding onto her, that it seemed as if I'd put my arm around her, when all I'd meant to do was steady her when she fell against me. I let it fall to my side but she didn't step away. It was as if we were frozen there, not moving. It probably only lasted for a matter of seconds, but it felt way longer than that.

"You want to kiss me, don't you?" she asked suddenly.

"No," I denied at once, though it wasn't completely true. The thought had come, unwelcome, to me just seconds before, and I wondered if she could somehow read my mind.

"Yes you do," she said, but she stepped back, turned, and started walking quickly toward the horses, calling their names.

I followed, thinking maybe I should tell her one more time that I did *not* want to kiss her. It wouldn't do to have her getting any fool ideas in her head. When I caught up with her, though, she was already offering sugar cubes to Century, and passed me some for Whisper.

No sense bringing it up again, I decided. *Best just to forget the whole subject.*

"I love the smell of horses," she said, running her hand along Century's neck. She pressed her face against him then, closing her eyes. She was murmuring things, soft and low, to the horse.

I fed Whisper the cubes Rhonda had given me, then realized I should soon be getting back to Grandpa's place.

"I gotta go," I said.

She opened her eyes, looking almost startled, as if she'd forgotten I was there. "Okay," she said. "See ya."

I walked back to Grandpa's place, arriving just in time for the meal Aunt Betty had made. It was roast chicken with mashed potatoes, carrots, stuffing, and gravy. Small bowls of different kinds of pickles that she'd made last summer were laid out among the main dishes.

Still full after the cake, I took small helpings, which made Aunt Betty fuss over me in her usual way.

"Land sakes, Cole," she said, "that can't be all you're going to eat. Why, when your father was your age, he near ate us out of house and home. Couldn't fill him up. Your grandfather used to say he had a hollow leg."

I'd heard about the hollow leg before and knew what was coming after it. Sure enough, she launched into the story about a summer fair when my father had been about sixteen and entered a pie eating contest.

"His face was covered, and I do mean covered, with berries. Blueberries, raspberries, strawberries. Looked like he'd been in some sort of terrible accident, he did."

I listened politely as she went on, describing how much pie each of the contestants had eaten, and how close my dad came to winning, how he *would* have won, if it wasn't for the fact that he'd had a full meal not long before the contest.

"Land sakes, child! What ever is the matter?"

I thought the new outburst was directed at me, and couldn't quite figure out what it was about. Then I realized she was looking at Jessie, seated beside me.

There was my little sister, pushing her food around her plate with a fork, tears running down her face.

"Penelope is gone," she said in a choked whisper. "I'm never going to see her again."

If my appetite hadn't met with Aunt Betty's approval before that, it didn't even exist afterward.

CHAPTER NINETEEN

I hadn't expected to have all this guilt over that stupid doll, but Jessie's heartbreak was getting harder and harder to take. More than once, I wished I'd never hid Penelope in Cassie's carriage. I even started wondering how I might be able to get it back. Then, something happened that made it even worse.

It was the next Wednesday evening. Jessie had gone off to bed — without even arguing — and Mom and Dad called me into the living room.

"We've been thinking about this whole thing with Wayne," Mom said, "and we were wondering if maybe we weren't a bit too harsh."

She went on then, telling me that they'd decided they hadn't been fair about the whole thing.

"Naturally, we don't approve of what happened a few weeks back, but Wayne is your best friend," she said.

"Has been for years," Dad said, nodding.

"Yes, and, well, we're sorry for taking such a hard line about it. So, you can let him know that he's welcome here again, though we don't expect a repeat of that episode."

"Anyway, I'm sure the two of you have learned from the experience," Dad added.

"You know," Mom went on, "seeing how distraught poor Jessie has been over her doll's disappearance kind of opened my eyes."

I looked at her questioningly, wondering how the two things were related.

"I realized that if she was that upset over losing a doll, it must be a hundred times worse for you to lose a friend."

I could hardly believe my ears. They were letting me hang out with Wayne again partly because I'd gotten rid of Penelope, though, of course, they didn't know that.

"Well?" Mom was looking at me quizzically. "Aren't you happy about it?"

"Uh, yeah, sure," I mumbled. I felt like the biggest lowlife ever. "Thanks."

"I was just telling Mona today how important friendship is. Mona, I said, a true friend is too precious to just throw away, especially for a man like Parnell."

It took me a few seconds to realize that she had crossed over into her soap opera world again. It was the first time I could remember her saying she *talked* to the characters. I glanced at Dad, to see if he found it scary too, but he didn't seem to realize what was going on.

"Those people aren't real, Mom," I said quietly.

She gave me a sharp glance.

"I mean, you can't actually talk to the characters on TV."

"I know that," she said with a weak smile. "I'm just giving you an example."

I shrugged, but I still thought it was kind of creepy. In spite of what she'd said, it was like she didn't always have a clear line drawn between reality and what went on in those stupid soaps.

It was still early, and Dad told me I could drop over to Wayne's place for a while if I wanted, but I'd worked that day and had to be at the shop at nine the next morning too. I decided I'd just turn in. I'd just crawled into bed and picked up the book I was reading when Mom knocked on my door.

"Phone," she said. "It's that girl again."

I hauled on my jeans and went to the kitchen thinking I'd be able to tell Wayne he didn't have to get his sister to call anymore.

"Hi," I said.

"Cole?" It wasn't Wayne.

"Yeah?"

"This is Rhonda."

Right away, I got this weird feeling in my gut, kind of like indigestion, I guess.

"What do you want?" It sounded as if I was mad that she was calling, which wasn't the way I meant to come across. I felt like an idiot.

"Some of us are going to the show on Friday." She either didn't notice, or ignored, the rude sound of my question. "I thought you might like to come with us."

I wondered if she meant for us to go as a couple, like a date or something, or if it was just a group thing. I was turning this over in my head when she spoke again.

"If you're not busy or anything, I mean."

"Oh, yeah, I mean, no." My tongue felt all thick and didn't seem to want to cooperate. "Uh, I'm not busy."

"Well, do you *want* to go?"

"Like, with *you*?"

"With all of us," she spoke slowly, as if she was explaining it to a small child. A small, dumb child.

"Okay." By that point, all I wanted was for the conversation to be over.

"Great then. We're meeting there at seven. In the lobby."

"Okay," I repeated, like a moron.

"Well, I'll see you there then."

"Okay." Apparently, that was the only word I could get out at the moment.

She said goodbye and hung up, but I swear I heard her start to laugh just before the click signalled the end of the call.

I couldn't concentrate on my book after that because I kept getting all these images in my head of Rhonda, the way she'd looked so peaceful when she was resting her face against Century, and the feeling I'd had when she was leaning up against me.

It's not like I'm crazy about her or anything, but I guess she's okay for a girl. I kept wondering what it would have been like to kiss her, and almost wishing I had. The whole thing was doing weird things to me.

When I finally fell asleep, I found myself dreaming about her. We were in the field with the horses and Rhonda was dancing in twirling movements around me, laughing and asking if I wanted to kiss her. I kept saying that I didn't, but I really did.

Then she tripped, and fell against me in slow motion, her hair brushing against my face. She smiled up at me, her eyes all wide and shining, and lifted her mouth until it almost touched mine. I had my arms around her and I could feel how warm and soft she was against me. That was when we kissed, and it was like an electric shock buzzed through me.

I woke up then, heart pounding and feeling oddly embarrassed. This was the first time I'd had a dream like that about a specific girl. It made me kind of dread facing Rhonda, though, of course, there was no way she could know anything about it.

Anyway, I couldn't even tell for sure if she liked me. Most girls go on so foolish that it's more than obvious. Not her. I didn't even know, when she'd asked if I wanted to kiss her, if she had wanted me to or if she was just making fun of me.

Like I said before, I'm not all gone on her or anything, but I wouldn't mind if she gave me some kind of hint one way or the other. Just in case.

CHAPTER TWENTY

It was sure hard to think about my work on Friday, what with all the stuff going on in my head. For one, I hadn't called Wayne yet, and couldn't quite figure out what was keeping me from letting him know that my folks had changed their minds about that whole situation.

I think I was still disgusted over the way he was using Lisa, and how hurt she was bound to be when she realized it. Wayne isn't a bad guy or anything, but he doesn't always stop to worry about other people. To tell the whole truth, I knew, deep down inside, that even if I pointed it out to him, he'd just call me a girl and laugh it off.

In any case, I'd let it slide for the time being.

Then there was Jessie and her doll, not to mention Rhonda and the way I kept thinking about her. But the thing that was bothering me the most was Sam.

It was becoming pretty clear to me that Sam's headaches weren't normal. It seemed he was having them nearly all the time too, since every time I turned around he was taking his pills. Besides that, he wasn't doing his work the way he normally did. He'd sit and stare at something he was supposed to be fixing, just stare for hours without lifting a finger, like he'd gone into a trance.

Since Sam's not the most approachable guy in the world, so I'd kept my mouth shut about the whole thing. But then this week I'd also noticed that he was hardly eating anything either, and his already thin frame was starting to look almost skeletal.

However he reacted, I knew it was time I said something. I waited for a quiet time that afternoon and took the bull by the horns.

"Sam," I said, clearing my throat and looking him right in the eye, "this may not be any of my business, but I'm worried about you."

"That so?" he grunted, half mocking.

"Yes, it *is* so. These headaches of yours, they're getting worse. I think you should see a doctor."

"Do you now?"

"Well, sure. There could be something wrong. You should go see about it."

Sam lifted his head and stared at me for a long minute. Then he reached into his shirt pocket and pulled out the pill bottle.

"Think I just bought these over the counter?" he asked.

I felt a bit foolish looking at the bottle. I should have realized before that it was a prescription of some sort.

"Oh," I said. "So you *have* seen a doctor."

"Yep."

"But you're not eating right either," I blurted after a pause, remembering my other concern.

"Ain't hungry."

"Yeah, but Sam, you have to eat. You're going to get really sick if you don't."

He chuckled, like I'd made a joke or something. "Don't you have work to do?" he asked, when he'd stopped. "Or am I paying you to pester me?"

I figured I'd tried. There wasn't anything else I could do; if Sam was going to be stubborn and stupid about it, there was no sense wasting my breath.

I busied myself organizing some shelves when I wasn't waiting on customers. For the past while I'd handled most of the sales and orders, while Sam had concentrated on the repairs. He was getting behind, though, since it was taking him so long to get anything done.

Just before six, when I was getting off work for the day, I had another idea.

"Say, Sam," I asked innocently, "do you have any relatives around here?"

"Nope."

"Nobody at all, huh?"

He glanced at me shrewdly. "Why? You figurin' to get someone else on my back?"

"'Course not," I lied. That was *exactly* what I'd been thinking.

"Just curious, are you?" he smirked.

"Yeah, well, actually, no. You were right. You aren't taking care of yourself, Sam. I thought that since you won't listen to me, you might listen to a family member."

Sam sighed then, and seemed to be thinking hard about something. "Look, kid," he said after a bit, "I guess maybe I should be straight with you. First off, though, I gotta know if I can trust you."

"Sure you can," I said.

"Like, if I tell you something, it's between the two of us. Goes no further."

"I promise."

"Truth is," Sam said without looking at me, "I ain't takin' these here pills for headaches. It's something else."

A horrible feeling came over me, and I knew right off that whatever he was about to tell me wasn't going to be good.

"It's cancer. Started in the stomach, but it's pretty well gone through me. 'Fraid I ain't got long."

"Can't they *do* anything?"

"Might've if they'd caught it earlier," he said matter-of-factly. "Don't make much difference now."

"But, what about chemo or radiation or something?"

"Too late. Oh, the doctor suggested a few things, but I looked him right in the eye and asked him to level with me, you know, tell me what the chances were if I put myself through all that. He admitted it wasn't going to do much, except maybe buy me a bit of time."

"Wouldn't that be better than nothing?"

"Not in old Sam's books, it wouldn't. Some of them cures are worse than what's killing a person in the first place."

I stood there like I was frozen in place, a dozen things running through my head and not one of them worth saying. Sam was dying. It seemed impossible, but I guess that was only because I'd just found out and hadn't had time to let it sink in.

I wanted to ask how long he had left, but it didn't seem the sort of question you could blurt out. As if he'd read my mind, Sam spoke again.

"This'll be my last summer. I got my mind made up that I ain't spending my last days hooked up to a bunch of tubes in the hospital either. No sir."

"But, won't you need to be taken care of, later on when it gets too bad for you to handle on your own with pills?"

"I'll be handling the end with pills all right," he said simply. "In my own time and in my own way."

I knew right off that he was talking about taking an overdose, and felt like I should say something about that, but nothing came to me.

"Now, don't you forget that this is between us, Cole," Sam said. "Last thing a man wants is a bunch of phonies coming around acting nice. Folks been calling me a no-good so-and-so my whole life." He grinned then. "I worked hard for that, and I don't aim to give it up now."

"But you're not actually like that," I insisted. "You're really a good guy."

"Glad you think so," he chuckled, "but I'm afraid that's not the popular opinion."

I knew that was true. I'd seen a side of Sam that other people didn't, and I couldn't help wondering why he'd spent his whole life the way he had. It seemed as though he'd been putting on an act, being real grouchy and short with folks, when underneath it, he wasn't that way at all. At least, he hadn't been with me, once I'd gotten to know him.

"Now, I ain't paying you overtime, so no need to hang around any longer," he said gruffly, breaking into my thoughts.

"See you tomorrow, then," I said. "And don't worry. Your secret's safe with me."

Thinking about Sam and what he'd just told me occupied my thoughts all the way home. It was only after I'd eaten that I remembered about the movie and Rhonda.

CHAPTER TWENTY-ONE

It was a good thing I had plans that evening, because I'd just discovered that keeping what Sam had just told me to myself wasn't as easy as you'd think. Don't get me wrong, I'm no rat. I can keep a secret as well as the next guy, but this was different. It weighed on me like some kind of burden that seemed almost too heavy to carry.

It wasn't as if I wanted to tell someone for the sake of gossiping. Nothing like that. I just wished I could get some input from my folks, sort of find out what they'd do in my situation. Here I was, apparently the only person besides Sam's doctor who knew he was dying. It seemed there ought to be something I should do, but I had no idea what that might be.

A couple of times I started thinking up scenarios I could tell my folks without actually coming out with the real story. Anything I thought of sounded too phoney, like the "I have a friend with a problem" stories that everyone can see right through.

"Is anything wrong, Cole?" Mom asked, interrupting my thoughts while we were eating. When Mom isn't parked in front of the TV, she's pretty observant.

"No, why?" I asked, wondering, as I usually did when she notices stuff, what the giveaway was.

"You seem distracted."

It was the vague kind of answer I'd expected. Mom isn't in the habit of explaining how she manages to pick up on that sort of thing. I figure that mothers have some kind of antenna that starts humming when something's up with their kids. She didn't pry any further, though, when I denied that anything was bothering me.

Like I said, it wasn't until we'd finished eating that I remembered the movie. Funny how I'd thought about nothing else for days and then it had gone right out of my head when Sam told me he was dying.

"Some of us are going to the show tonight," I said after the chores were done. I tried to keep my voice real casual, so Mom wouldn't launch into one of her interrogations. It didn't work.

"Oh? Who all is going?" she asked right away, looking at me carefully.

"Just some kids."

"Is Wayne going?"

"No. I mean, I don't think so." It seemed unlikely,

since Rhonda isn't what you'd call fond of Wayne. Truth is, she can't stand him, and makes no effort to pretend otherwise. He says it's just a cover to hide the fact that she really wants him.

"Well, then who?"

"I don't know. I mean, I don't know *exactly* who's going to be there. Just a bunch of us."

She looked at me suspiciously. "Well, who invited you?"

"What difference does it make?" I was getting a bit tired of the questions.

"Was it that girl who's been calling you?"

I should have known she'd put two and two together. I changed the subject by claiming I was going to be late and had to hurry, which wasn't a lie. As I went toward my room to get ready, I heard her telling Dad that she was pretty sure I had a date.

"With a girl," she added in a loud whisper.

"Well, I should hope so," he said dryly.

"He won't tell me who," she complained, ignoring the sarcasm.

"Maybe we should torture it out of him," Dad suggested. "Or maybe we could just let him be. I imagine he'll tell us when he's ready."

I silently thanked Dad for sticking up for me, especially since I knew that Mom would sulk all evening over the fact that he hadn't taken her side.

There wasn't much time to get ready so I took a really quick shower and threw on some fresh clothes. After brushing my teeth, I noticed Dad's aftershave sitting by the sink, and decided to put on a bit. I wondered if I'd overdone it when I passed through the living room on my way to the door and Mom's head bounced up. She was sniffing the air when I left, but at least she didn't say anything.

I was a few minutes late getting to the theatre. As soon as I went through the door I saw Rhonda standing with a group of kids from school. She was talking and laughing and didn't notice me until I walked over. That seemed to answer my question about whether or not we were sort of supposed to be together. After all, wouldn't she have been watching for me if that was the case? I told myself I didn't care.

"Oh, hi." She turned and smiled at me then. "You made it."

"Yeah." I smiled back, feeling suddenly happy. She sure looked glad to see me. Maybe we *were* together. I said hello to the others, noticing that they all seemed to be paired off.

"Get your ticket yet?"

"Uh, not yet."

"Better hurry up. We're almost ready to go in."

I got a ticket, then went back over.

"You want some popcorn or anything? Something to drink?"

"If you're getting a drink, I'll just have a few sips later on, if that's okay."

"Sure." I was halfway to the counter when I realized I hadn't found out what kind of pop she liked. I went back and asked.

"Anything at all," she said. She touched my arm with her hand.

We are *together*, I decided as I joined the queue for treats. I ordered the largest Pepsi they had, then got some licorice, chocolate-coated peanuts, and a large popcorn. I didn't want her to think I was cheap, and she might get hungry later.

"Your folks starving you?" Rhonda giggled when I got back to the group with my hands full.

"Hey, when you have muscles like I do, you have to eat a lot to maintain them."

"Sorry. I should have realized," she laughed.

"After all, a guy never knows when he might have to fight off a pack of wolves."

Laughing harder, she stepped into line beside me as we passed in our tickets and went into the theatre where our movie was about to begin.

The previews were already showing as we took our seats. Rhonda was to my right. She glanced at me with a smile every now and then. I felt ridiculously happy.

Normally, when I go to a movie, I find myself drawn right into it. Not this time. Later on, I hardly remembered a thing about it, except it was some kind of action show with the usual romance thrown in. I guess producers have to do that for the females in the audience.

Some of the couples around us were already kissing by the time the main attraction had been on for a few minutes. I'd finally admitted to myself that I wanted to kiss Rhonda too, but she was sitting straight up, watching the screen intently.

I noticed, then, that she had her hand resting on her leg beside me. I wondered if I was supposed to take hold of it. With half the supplies from the concession stand in my hands, that wasn't going to be easy. Trying to be casual about it, I lowered the popcorn bag to the floor and let the other snacks drop to my lap.

It took what seemed like half the movie to let my hand slide over to hers. When they finally touched, I nearly jumped because it felt like a bolt of electricity shot through me.

Rhonda turned her head and gave me what I took for an encouraging smile, but I was too stunned from the unexpected reaction to do more than just sit there. After a few moments of this, I felt her fingers move gently over mine.

I told myself it was now or never. Panic rushed over me. I grabbed her hand as if I was capturing and subduing it. She made no effort to pull away. I stared hard at the movie.

Barely moving for the rest of the show, I kept telling myself I could do it, but I knew that I'd used up all my nerve and was never going to be able to lean over and kiss her. When it ended, we stood and filed out with the others. A moment later, Jeff arrived to pick her up and Rhonda hardly glanced at me before she got into her dad's truck and disappeared.

I felt like a total loser.

CHAPTER TWENTY-TWO

I dreaded getting home that night, knowing full well that Mom would be there, waiting to pounce. She'd had a few hours to brood over her lack of success in dragging information out of me, and was sure to have formulated a new way to interrogate me.

Thinking about this, I almost missed seeing the small, bent figure sitting on a bench in the town park. Hardly anyone ever goes there in the evenings, though it's common to see young mothers there with their kids during the daytime.

As I passed by, I could see that it was a girl, and there was something familiar about her. I walked closer, to get a better look, and saw that it was Lisa Manderson. Normally, I'd have just kept going, but her posture caught my attention. The way she was doubled over, it looked as if she might be hurt.

"Hey, Lisa," I said, approaching her.

"Oh, hi, Cole," she answered, bringing her head up and sniffing.

Alarmed, I could see that she'd been crying, and I wished I'd minded my own business. Now, I was trapped.

"You okay?" It was a stupid question, I knew. Her eyes were red and puffy and her face was blotchy. Any moron could see she wasn't okay.

She nodded, which made her look even more forlorn. "Yes, I'm okay," she said, then burst into tears.

"No, you're not." I sat beside her on the bench. "You're upset."

"It's my own fault."

"How's that?"

"I should have known better." Her voice quivered, giving her words a bleating sound. She swallowed hard and took a deep breath.

I knew, sure as I was sitting there, that it was something to do with Wayne. I stayed quiet, hoping she wouldn't tell me any more about it, but she didn't need any encouragement.

"I *hate* him," she whispered, gulping air.

"It'll be okay," I offered lamely.

"He was *using* me," she lamented, "and I let him. I feel so stupid."

As disloyal as it seemed to stay there and listen, escape was impossible. I tried to say something neutral, knowing full well there was no steering this conversation in another direction.

"*You're* his best friend," Lisa said, her eyes widening with the realization. It sounded like she was accusing me of something horrible.

"Yeah, well …"

"What do I care?" Her eyes snapped with sudden anger. "He's a pig and a liar. And I *hate* him."

Silence settled for a moment. Lisa sagged, as though the effort of saying this much had taken all her energy. I tried to think of some reason to tell her I had to get going, before she regained momentum. My mind was blank.

"I got in a lot of trouble," she went on after a bit. "Do you know what he got me to do?"

I knew all right, but I couldn't exactly admit this to her.

"Steal from my own parents!" Anguish filled her voice and I was afraid she might start crying again. "And I did it, because I thought he liked me. Then, I got caught."

"What happened?" I asked automatically.

"Oh, you know, big freak-out. Lots of yelling and stuff. I got grounded for a month."

I wondered how come she was out, if she was grounded.

"I didn't care about any of that," she went on. "Because I had Wayne, you know? It didn't matter if

I was in trouble or not, as long as I was going out with him."

"You were *going out* with Wayne?" I was shocked, and it came through in my tone of voice.

"Well, I *thought* I was." She levelled a look at me. "I guess it was just wishful thinking. He called me regular, you know, and he *acted* like we were going out, even if he didn't actually ask me."

"Uh-huh." That sounded like Wayne, all right.

"So, anyway, I saw him a few times, and I brought liquor from my dad's cabinet." She cleared her throat. "He *asked* me to. Said we'd have a lot of fun together, but I never spent more than an hour with him each time, before he had to go somewhere. I believed what I wanted to believe. I, you know, *convinced* myself that he really liked me and he honestly had to go places.

"But he was just getting rid of me." Lisa lifted her chin and stared straight ahead with this admission. It seemed that talking about it was calming her, though, since she no longer looked like she was going to burst out crying.

"I'm glad I got caught," she said quietly. "My dad had noticed that some of the bottles were missing, and yesterday when I took another one, he stopped me when I was coming out of the room.

"He and mom sat me down and gave me this big screaming lecture, and went on that I should see a counsellor. You know, because they assumed I was drinking this stuff myself. I don't even *like* it."

She made a face to back this up. "Well, Wayne was furious! I couldn't even call him to tell him what had happened, so there he was waiting for me, and I didn't show up. When I finally had a chance to phone him today, he told me to sneak out tonight, and meet him. And, of course, to bring booze.

"I was so naïve! I thought he was mad because he'd wanted to see me, and maybe partly because I was in trouble. Well, I sure found out different a while ago."

I could picture the scene even before she described it.

"I got out of the house all right, but I couldn't get anything to take with me. Dad locked it all up after the scene the other day. Still, I didn't think that was a big deal. I figured we'd just hang out, spend some time together. When I showed up without anything for him to drink though, and told him about it being locked up, he flipped out. And he told me to get lost and called me ..."

Her voice trailed off then, but I had no trouble filling in the blanks. I'd already heard Wayne refer to Lisa as a pig's arse and a bowser. As awful as it seemed, I knew full well he'd said something similar right to her face. Being ticked off like that, he wouldn't even hesitate.

"Listen, Lisa," I said, "you're a nice girl. Too good for a jerk like Wayne."

I thought he was your best friend." She looked at me in surprise.

"Yeah, he was." I realized I'd used the past tense, but didn't correct myself. "But that doesn't mean I agree with everything he does. What he did to you was cruel, and it's even worse to know that he couldn't care less how you felt. My advice is to chalk this up to experience and forget him. You'll find someone a lot better, believe me."

"I really liked him," she said with a catch in her voice. "A lot."

"Maybe he did you a favour in a way, by showing you what he's really like," I said. "Anyway, I'd better get going,"

I was about to get up and take off when I noticed that she had a worried look on her face, so I asked if there was a problem.

"Oh, nothing, really. I was just wondering how I'm going to get back in the house, without getting caught." She made a wry face. "I'm already in enough trouble."

"How were you planning to get in?"

"Well, I thought Wayne was going to be with me, and he could have boosted me up to my window. I can get out it without help, but I can't get back in. It's too high."

"I'll go with you," I offered. "I hope your folks haven't noticed that you're gone."

We walked to her place and went along the hedge that borders the yard until we were alongside her window. I felt kind of strange lifting her up so she could scramble inside. It seemed as though I was doing something wrong, holding Lisa like that, as if it was a betrayal to Rhonda.

Once Lisa was inside, she turned and stuck her head out.

"Thanks, Cole, for everything," she whispered. "I owe you big time."

"It was nothing," I said.

"No, I mean it. If there's ever anything I can do for you, you just let me know."

An idea came to me.

"You know, Lisa, I think there *is* something."

CHAPTER TWENTY-THREE

Saturday was a slow day at the shop, which was just as well, since Sam was feeling lousy. He admitted he was taking more of the pills the doctor had prescribed, and they made him kind of woozy.

"I have to cut back," he said in a slow, dreamy voice, at one point in the day.

"Why should you? I mean, if they help the pain, what's the difference?"

"Can't get my work done," he mumbled. "And I need to get things in order."

"I can help," I said, though I doubted there was much I could really do. After all, I knew nothing about repairing the various things that local men brought to Sam.

But Sam agreed — though at first I thought he was just being polite. Then he told me to go into the back room and get down the books. I knew right away what he was talking about. There were piles and piles of hard, black books stuffed on the top shelves of the storage units out there.

"Where will I put them?" I asked.

Sam seemed unable to think that through. He looked at me as if I'd asked him to solve the mystery of the sphinx or something.

"I could clear off the big table out back," I suggested after a moment. He nodded, and I spent the next hour removing the piles of odds and ends and finding new places for them. It was no small task, since that table served as an overflow, and most of the shelves were already full. In the end, I filled a couple of boxes and used a marker to record the contents of each one. The bare surface, when it finally appeared, was covered in grime.

The table probably hadn't been cleaned since the day it was put there, and a lot of the stains, like oil, didn't come off. I did the best I could, then got the ladder out and started getting the books down.

I wiped thick layers of dust off them before piling them in neat stacks.

"Okay, they're all there," I told Sam when I was finished.

"Need to sort them out," he said heavily.

"Like, by year?"

"Year, and business," he nodded. "Kept my personal records here too. Should take those home."

I saw what he meant as soon as I started going through the books. For each year, there was one for the business, and one with ledgers of all Sam's expenses at home. Every deposit and expense was recorded in thickly printed letters.

It was time-consuming to get them all sorted, since they spanned the last forty-eight years. I had an idea when I was partway through, and started labelling them by year with a whiteout pen, writing the numbers in small letters on the spine of each book.

By closing time that afternoon, I was done.

"If you'd put the house books in my car, I'd be obliged," Sam said approvingly when he'd surveyed my work.

"You taking them home?"

"Yep."

"I'll come with you," I said. "Carry them into the house for you, and put them wherever you want them."

He looked like he was about to protest, then thought better of it and said that would be fine. I carried them all out and then slipped into the passenger seat, wondering if Sam should even be driving in his drugged condition. He took it slow, though, apparently aware that his reflexes weren't at their best.

Once we got to his place, he stood in the hallway for a few moments. It was clear that he was having trouble deciding where they should go, not because it was a difficult thing to figure out, but because his brain wasn't working normally. It was sad to see him looking lost and confused that way. I waited patiently, then suggested the spare bedroom would be a good place.

"Spare room," he repeated. I took that as agreement and carried the books, an armload at a time, and stacked them along the wall.

"All done," I said, walking into the living room afterward. Sam was seated in a big easy chair, fast asleep.

Poor old guy, I thought. Who knew how hard it was for him to keep going, day by day, working in the shop while cancer ate away at him relentlessly? He was probably exhausted by the time he got home each evening. No wonder he wasn't eating right, he was using the bit of energy he had left just to keep the shop going.

I found some blankets in a hall closet and covered Sam up with one after hauling his boots off. The sun was shining on his face, so I closed the curtains too. Before leaving, I had an idea, and went to the fridge.

There wasn't much in there — the usual bologna and mustard, a carton of eggs, some cheese and milk. The cupboards held stacks of canned beans, soups, and vegetables. A loaf of bread sat on the counter, and the freezer was empty except for a bag of frozen peas and a tray of ice, long eroded.

The sink was piled with pots and dishes, most of them crusted with dried food particles. As quietly as possible, I stacked them on the counter and filled the sink with hot, soapy water. While the dishes soaked, I washed off the counters and the small chrome table, where Wayne and I had sat just a few short weeks ago.

Once the dishes were done, I checked on Sam again. He was snoring softly, his face slack with the relief of temporary escape from pain. I scrawled a note urging him to try to eat something, then slipped out the door and headed home.

As I walked along, I might as well admit that I was fighting tears. Wayne would have said I was being a girl, but it somehow didn't bother me that I felt like crying. There was Sam, old and alone, suffering and staring death in the face, without one person in the world who cared. Except me.

It was a surprise to realize *how much* I cared, considering how I'd felt about him when I first started working at the shop. Maybe it was because of how he'd helped me and Wayne out the night we showed up at his place. When I thought of that now, I knew what that must have cost him, considering how sick he was and all. To have two young lads arrive at your door at that hour and in that condition, and to do what he did even though he was in constant pain, well, it was an act of kindness you just wouldn't expect.

I thought of Grandpa's words, how he always said you never really know a man until you work for him, and I thought of how true they were.

Sam Kerrigan, widely known as hateful and miserable, was really a good and decent man.

And a friend of mine.

Chapter Twenty-four

It was Lisa who'd pointed out the problem with my request when we'd had our whispered conversation at her window that night.

"But I'm grounded," she'd reminded me, once she heard what I wanted her to do.

"Oh, yeah. Sorry, I forgot." I smiled, to show her I wasn't a jerk like Wayne, just wanting to use her. "It's okay."

"No, wait." She glanced backward as she spoke, as if she was afraid she was going to get caught talking out her window. That struck me as kind of funny, considering she'd just taken a much bigger chance by sneaking out of the house.

Of course, she wasn't nuts about me. Wayne must have seemed worth the risk, until she'd found out the truth.

"I can do it," she said. "My folks will be out on Sunday afternoon. They play bridge with the Johnsons every Sunday. They'll be gone for hours."

"What if they call, and you don't answer the phone?"

"That'll never happen. Not when they're playing bridge. It's like a religion to them; they'd never stop the game to make a call."

"If you're sure." I wasn't completely convinced.

"It'll be a piece of cake. Assuming I can find her. Where will I meet you afterward?"

"I'll wait for you at Tessa's." Tessa's was a small diner on Princess Street. "What time?"

"My folks leave around one-thirty. I'll wait fifteen minutes, just in case they come back. My mom is *always* forgetting things! It shouldn't take me more than half an hour, so be at the diner a little after two and I'll get there as soon as I can."

"Any idea *how* you're going to do it?"

"Not yet," she said. "I'll figure something out though, don't worry."

"Okay, but don't take any chances. If you don't show up, I'll know something went wrong."

Just before I left, Lisa leaned out the window and kissed me on the cheek and told me I was a really nice guy. It seemed the kind of thing a person has to respond to, so I told her she was a really nice girl too.

Real original, huh? That seemed to create a sudden awkwardness between us, and as I shifted from foot to foot, she slipped inside, giving me a little wave.

I could hardly sit still through church on Sunday morning, all nervous and worried about the whole thing. I went back and forth from wishing I hadn't asked her to do it to hoping she succeeded. Images of her getting caught kept coming to me, filling me with guilt, even though nothing had happened yet.

By the time we'd eaten lunch I was a wreck. You'd have thought it was me taking the chance instead of Lisa. I left the house a little after one, too antsy to sit at home and wait.

It's funny, how you can think of all these things that could go wrong, but if something does, it usually turns out to be something entirely unexpected. I'd been walking around for a half an hour or so, when I heard my name being called.

"Hey," I answered, turning and trying to hide my dismay.

"What's up, dude? Your mom still being weird?"

"Uh, no, actually. I was going to call you to let you know my folks changed their minds."

"Excellent." Wayne smirked. "I knew you'd get them to see the error of their ways."

"I didn't do anything," I said. "They just decided on their own."

"Whatever. So, let's go down to the quarry. I have something to show you."

"I can't. I mean, not right now."

"What's with you anyway, Cole? I swear, you've turned into such a *girl* this summer."

"I have to do something, that's all."

"Running errands for Mommy?" he mocked in a falsetto voice.

"Knock it off, Wayne. I said I have something to do, and that's it. I don't have to explain anything to you."

"Eeeww! I'd better be careful the girl doesn't try to smack me," he laughed, lifting both hands and slapping the air in front of him.

"I gotta go," I said, and started to walk away. It was close to two o'clock by then, and I didn't want to be late.

"Yo, wait up, man."

I didn't know what to do when he fell into step beside me. There was no way I could have him with me when Lisa showed up, but I had no idea how I was going to get rid of him. Wayne's the sort that would stick around just to be a jerk, if he thought I had something to hide — which I did. If I told him I was meeting a girl, he'd hang around for sure, to see who it was.

We'd almost reached Tessa's by then. My guts were in a turmoil like you wouldn't believe, and a hundred things were going through my head at once. I finally decided to tell him I'd go to the quarry after all, thinking I could always call Lisa later and tell her I hadn't been able to get out.

"You said you had something to show me at the quarry?"

"Yeah." His face lit up triumphantly. "Wait 'till you see it, dude. You're gonna …"

"No, I'm not gonna anything." The gloating look on his face had made me suddenly furious.

"*What?*"

"I said no. I'm not going there. Not now."

Wayne had seen that I was about to cave in, and the unexpected change caused an instant rage in him. His face clouded with anger, and I could see he was winding up to tell me off.

"Here's the thing, Wayne," I said, before he could speak. "I'm sick of the way you act. Really sick of it. You push people around, you put me down constantly, and you seem to think the only person in the world who counts is you. Well, you're wrong. And I've had enough.

"Another thing. I could have called you a few days ago, but I didn't. And you know why? Because I didn't *want* to." I hadn't thought that through until that moment, but as soon as the words were out, I knew it was the truth.

Wayne's eyes were on me, hard and full of cold fury. I'd never talked to him that way before, not even when we argued about something. Expecting him to start yelling, or maybe even hit me, I was surprised when he didn't move or speak.

I'd been about to go on, and there was a lot more that I suddenly wanted to say, but I didn't. Instead, I ended it there, like that, and turned to walk away, making sure my steps were slow and even so he wouldn't think I was afraid of him.

The fact of the matter was, I'd always been kind of afraid of Wayne. Realizing that had been part of the anger I'd felt in finally standing up to him. It wasn't fear of *him*, exactly, even though I knew if we ever got into a fight he'd probably win. No, it was another kind of fear. All through the years I'd gone along, done what he wanted, pushed aside misgivings, because I knew, somewhere inside, that if I didn't, we wouldn't even *be* friends.

I was half a block away when I heard him, and again, it wasn't what I'd expected. There was no shouting or threats, no putdowns or anything like that. Rather, he started laughing, and it was the kind of laugh that you'd hear from an insane person. It creeped me out so much that I almost started running.

It was a relief to turn the corner at Princess Street, and I hurried to Tessa's, anxious to get inside, out of sight, just in case he came along behind me. I slid into a corner booth where I could see outside, but wasn't visible to anyone passing by. When five minutes had gone by without a sign of him, I finally relaxed a bit.

A few minutes later I saw Lisa coming along the street. She opened the door too fast, making it bang and bringing Tessa out from the kitchen, where she cooks the food orders the waitresses take to her. Wiping her hands on an apron that covered her from neck to knee, she glared at Lisa, the kind of warning look that doesn't need words.

"Uh, sorry," Lisa said. "It was an accident."

She spied me then and hurried over to the booth. "Hey," she smiled. "I got it!"

As she spoke, she passed a blue plastic bag across the table. I peeked inside to make sure it was the right one, then asked how she'd done it.

"I'll tell you about it another time," Lisa said. "I want to get back home right away. You know, just in case."

I thanked her, paid for the Pepsi I'd ordered but hardly touched, and was out the door and on my way home less than a minute after she'd left.

CHAPTER TWENTY-FIVE

I stuck the plastic bag into the garbage on my way through the kitchen once I got home. The house was quiet and I figured Mom and Dad were having an afternoon nap, which is kind of funny when you think about it. I mean, you usually picture little kids needing naps in the daytime, but my folks often have one on Sunday if we don't go anywhere.

I went down the hall where the bedrooms and bathroom are, and found Jessie sitting on the edge of her bed. She was looking at a book and hardly glanced up when she saw me standing in the doorway.

"Hey, Jess," I said softly, "are the old folks sleeping?"

She shrugged and turned a page in her book.

"I just wondered because if they are, we don't want to make any noise and wake them up."

"Yeah?" she asked, clearly unable to understand why I was bothering her with that sort of comment.

"Well, anyway, I just wanted to mention that, so you'll know not to yell or anything when you see what I found."

With that, I pulled a hand from behind my back to show her what I held.

"Penelope!" she shrieked at the top of her lungs. I might have known my cautionary remarks were a waste of breath.

Hurling herself forward, she nearly knocked me over. She grabbed the doll and clutched it, her face alight with happiness. I was kind of happy myself, looking at her.

"Oh, Penelope, Penelope!" she cried, kissing the dumb thing's face. "I thought you were gone forever."

"Yeah, well, she's back," I said dryly, knowing full well that life was about to go back to normal at our place. Somehow, it didn't bother me. In fact, strange as it seems, I was glad.

"Where'd you find her?" Jessie asked when her excitement had faded a bit.

"Oh, a few streets over."

If she noticed that my answer was a bit evasive, she didn't press it.

"You two want a push on the swing or anything?" I asked. It seemed a good idea to get her out of the house, since she was sure to wake up Mom and Dad, if she hadn't already.

"Okay." She skipped down the hall and out the door into the yard. I followed along, enjoying the sight of her bouncing and talking a mile a minute to Penelope.

"Make us go high, Cole," Jessie commanded as she settled onto the swing, her arms looping the ropes and hugging the doll. "Penelope likes to go real high."

I pushed the two of them higher and higher, taking care to keep the swing even so it wouldn't start going wild. Jessie whooped in delight and told me that Penelope said I was doing a good job.

You know, as annoying as Jessie can be at times, it really doesn't take that much to make her happy. I decided, being older and everything, that I could learn to handle her a bit better, instead of letting her get on my nerves so easy. After all, I'm a working man, and just about completely grown up.

My arms were getting tired by the time Jessie yelled that Penelope wanted to get down now. I slowed the swing and steadied it once it was nearly stopped.

"Penelope is hungry," she announced. "Can you get us some cookies and milk?"

"Can't you …" I started to ask why she couldn't get her own darned milk and cookies.

"Sure. I could use a little snack myself," I said instead.

As we headed back into the house, Jessie did the weirdest thing. She slipped her hand into mine.

"Cole, thanks for finding Penelope," she said. For a girl who hardly ever talks lower than a bossy yell, her voice was all soft and shy.

For some reason, my throat was all tight and I couldn't quite speak. I just smiled at her and went to the cupboard to get some glasses. Pouring two tumblers full of milk, I dug out a bag of Oreos and carried it all to the table.

"Better make sure Penelope doesn't eat too many," I said. "Might spoil her appetite for dinner."

"We'll just have two," Jessie promised. She sat two cookies in front of the doll, two in front of herself, and proceeded to eat the four of them. As Dad would say, she's dumb like a fox sometimes. Once "they" were finished, they went to Jessie's room. I was informed that this was so Penelope could say hello to all the things she'd been lonesome for while she was away.

I'd just cleaned up the table when Mom came wandering down the hall, still looking a bit sleepy.

"Did I hear Jessie yell a while ago?" she asked. "I thought I heard her say Penelope."

"You did," I said. "I, uh, found the doll over on Princess Street."

"Really?" Mom looked at me real close. "Wasn't that lucky."

"Yeah." I wasn't sure if she was suspicious or if she just wasn't fully awake. "I took her outside with it, on the swing, so she wouldn't wake you, but I guess it was too late. She was pretty excited."

Mom seemed to be puzzling the whole thing through, but then she sort of shook her head, like it was beyond her. Or maybe she just decided it was one of those things that are better left alone. With mothers, who knows?

"Would you bring some potatoes up from the cold room, dear?" she asked. "I'm going to make some homemade fries and burgers for supper.

Mom's fries are the best, though we don't have them often, on account of she says we all have to watch our cholesterol. She scrubs the potatoes with a kind of wire brush, then slices and deep fries them. They're way better than the kind you get at fast food places, 'cause there's still a bit of skin on, which gives them a real good flavour.

I took the bowl she handed me and scooted down to the basement where we store vegetables and the different kinds of pickles that Mom makes after Grandpa's garden comes in. The shelves and bins were starting to get bare, but with a new crop coming, they'd soon be filled again. I like the pickles she makes, but I'm not crazy about the job I always get when she's making them, which is chopping onions.

The smell of hamburger patties sizzling on the barbeque was already drifting in the window when I got back upstairs. I helped Mom slice the potatoes into wedges and set the table as she dropped them into the fryer.

In no time, we were all sitting down to eat. Jessie and Penelope were across from me, seated in chairs side by side.

"Penelope wants you to take us for ice cream after supper, Cole," she announced.

I told her I had other plans, since I'd already decided I was going to drop over to Sam's place, just to see how he was doing.

"But, Cole," Jessie insisted with her mouth full of fries and ketchup, "Penelope *needs* ice cream!"

CHAPTER-SIX

You'd think that a guy who'd just ditched his best friend and returned a doll to his sister, knowing full well that she'd use it to torture him mercilessly, would be feeling kind of down, but I wasn't. In fact, in some ways, I felt better than I had in weeks.

Of course, there were still two things bothering me: Sam being sick and knowing I'd been such a failure on the date with Rhonda both kept coming at me kind of hard.

After I'd caved in and taken Jessie for the ice cream that Penelope *needed*, I decided that what *I* needed was to take a long walk. I still planned to pay a visit to Sam later, but I wanted to clear my head first.

I headed out to Preacher's Point, which is called that because they used to hold revival meetings there in the summers. Mom says her folks took her a few times when she was a kid, and that almost everyone in town would be there, swaying and singing along with the music, and listening to the travelling evangelists' urgent messages. She said it was like a huge picnic, only without the food, because everyone would visit after the meeting was over. That didn't sound like much of a picnic to me.

Anyway, the point, which edges the ocean, isn't used for anything much these days. The water is too shallow for swimming, unless you want to walk a long way out, and the beach is too boggy for sunbathing. To get to the beach, you have to go through a jungle of long, sharp grasses, and the air is pungent, which puts most people off. Not me. I always liked the marshy smell of the place, and had found a huge boulder that had a sort of ledge in it, which made a perfect seat. I go there when something's bothering me, and just sit and think.

It was a fine evening, and the sun, though starting to drop in the sky, still offered enough heat to warm my rock and give me that lazy feeling I so liked when I was there. It was real soothing.

Sometimes, when I go there, things kind of sort themselves out in my head. Even when they don't, I usually feel a lot better after lying back and letting things settle inside.

This evening, even though there were two things to mull over, I knew that only one had a possible solution. There wasn't a thing I could do about Sam. He was going to die and all the thinking and wishing in the world wouldn't change that. In spite of that, I'd had an idea, and needed to figure out how to approach it with him. Even though he's not so hard to talk to after all, there are some things that are off limits. I just didn't know if this might be one of them, or how he'd take it when I brought it up.

I knew from experience that it's not always a good idea to rehearse what you're going to say ahead of time. That can go either way — either you say a thing just the way you wanted to, or you bungle it real bad. It depends on the person you're talking to, and whether or not he lets you go ahead and get it out. If there's any interruption, I tend to get all confused, lose track of what I was saying, and end up sounding like a blithering idiot.

I guess I knew full well that Sam was the interrupting type. After thinking about it for a while, I decided I'd just broach the subject with him and then take it from there.

On the matter of Rhonda, I knew she was pretty disappointed about the way things had gone at the movie. That was clear enough from the way she'd left, not saying goodbye or anything, and just getting into her dad's truck and leaving without a backward glance. I could still see the back of her head, stiff and unflinching as she sat in the passenger seat. It didn't seem likely that she'd ever want another date with me.

I was pretty discouraged about the whole thing until a thought hit me. It was more like a question, really, but it sure changed the way I was feeling. Basically, it occurred to me to wonder *why* she was upset. From there, it wasn't hard to come up with an answer that made the whole thing seem better.

The only reason I could think of for her to have felt let down over the date was that she liked me. Otherwise, why would she have cared that I sat there like a stick? A girl wouldn't be disappointed over not being kissed unless she really *wanted* to be kissed.

That cheered me a lot, though I knew full well I might just be convincing myself of something I wanted to believe. In any case, I felt a whole lot better when I set out for Sam's house.

The place seemed unusually still and quiet when I found myself heading up the walk to his front door. It gave me a horrible start, even though there was no reason to think anything had happened. A huge sense of relief washed over me when, a moment after I'd knocked, the door swung open and Sam's face appeared.

"That you, Cole?" he peered at me.

"Yeah, it's me, Sam." His confusion cleared quickly, but it was sad to see how disoriented he'd been. I knew it must be the medication he was taking, affecting him like that.

"Well, I suppose you can come in, since you're here anyway."

It wasn't the most gracious invitation I've ever heard, but that didn't bother me. I'd gotten used to the way Sam acted, and had come to see it as just that — an act.

I followed him to the living room, noting that his shuffle was slower than normal. The way he moved, it was obvious that he was in pain.

"It's bad, isn't it?" I asked once we were seated, Sam in his big easy chair and me on the couch.

"Not so bad," he said. "Had a kidney stone once, years back. That was worse."

"You eat today?"

"I suppose I did." He seemed unsure, and pondered his answer. "Soup, maybe."

"That's good, Sam. Soup is good for you," I said. "You should try to eat a bit more though. You know, regular meals and stuff."

"You just come here to nag me like a woman, or you got something better to talk about?"

I cleared my throat, determined not to let him put me off, like he was clearly trying to do. I had to get to the reason I was there. "Look, Sam, there's something I wanted to talk about."

"You ain't changin' my mind," he said. His eyes wandered around the room. "Should have kept my mouth shut."

"No, I'm glad you told me." Alarm filled me, and I was afraid he was going to shut the conversation down before I could get to my point. "I know this is what you want. I'm not going to lie to you and say I agree with it, because I don't, but it's your decision."

The fact of the matter was that I'd been struggling with the whole thing ever since he'd told me about it. I'd seen the agony he was in much of the time, the thin coats of sweat on his face and the barely hidden grimaces that couldn't hide the pain. It was hard to fault him for wanting to end the suffering in his own time and way.

At the same time, I couldn't quite reconcile myself with the idea that suicide was justified, no matter what. A person is supposed to have faith, and on top of that, there are certain rules. God's rules. Breaking one like that had to be a big deal.

There was no time for moralizing just then, though, not with Sam staring me down.

"So, then, spit it out. What you came to say." His voice was gruff.

"I want to be with you, when you do it."

"You think I'm afraid?" he snorted. "Need someone to hold my hand?"

"No, nothing like that. I just don't want you to be alone, when the time comes."

"Hungh," Sam grunted. His head kind of sagged forward a bit, like the weight of what I'd just proposed was pulling him down. He sat like that without moving for a couple of long minutes before he said anything else, and then it didn't seem quite related to what we'd been talking about.

"They say there's a light. When you go."

"Yeah, I guess I've heard that."

"That's what they say, anyway." He seemed to be drifting off.

"Well, think about it, would you, Sam?" I stood. There didn't seem to be anything else to say at the moment.

He nodded, but I couldn't tell if he was agreeing or falling asleep. I started to leave the room, then this weird urge came over me. I didn't fight it, or even think it through. I just walked over to Sam, leaned down, and put my arms around his shoulders.

"You're my friend," I said hoarsely. "And, I love you."

At first, I wasn't sure if he'd heard me, since his eyes were closed by then. But I knew he had when I saw a tear trickle from the corner of one eye and make its way down his grizzled old cheek.

CHAPTER TWENTY-SEVEN

Sam never once mentioned our conversation as the next week went by. I figured he'd decided against taking me up on my offer, but there wasn't much I could do about it. To tell the truth, part of me was kind of relieved. Although the idea had seemed good at the time, second thoughts had begun to plague me. After all, I'd never been around anyone who'd died. Not at the actual moment of death anyway. I had no idea what it would really be like.

On the other hand, the thought of Sam slipping off to the next world without anyone there was real sad. He'd lived his whole life alone; it seemed wrong for him not to at least have someone with him at the end. Besides, what if he got scared, and changed his mind at the last minute?

Well, I told myself, *it's his decision*. There was no sense in pushing it. I did wonder, though, if he'd tell me when he was going to do it. Maybe not the exact time or whatever, but would he say goodbye somehow, the last time I saw him, so I'd know?

On Thursday morning, Sam was late getting to the shop, and I stood on the sidewalk with a cold feeling of dread in me. He hadn't said a word when I saw him home the night before, as I'd taken to doing every day. But with Sam, you never knew.

When he finally showed up, pulling his car into its usual place, I felt half weak with relief. I watched him get out, moving slowly and painfully along the sidewalk until he reached the door. He stuck the key into the lock without so much as a grunt in my direction, and we entered the shop in silence.

That's how we spent most of the day. I took care of the things that had become second nature to me by then — waiting on customers, keeping the place clean and tidy, and placing orders. It occurred to me at one point that, after Sam was gone, the things he'd ordered for people wouldn't get to them.

"I suppose we should stop taking orders before, uh, the shop is going to be closed for good," I said, not knowing how else to put it.

Sam seemed to consider this for a moment. "Folks need their orders," he said at last, as if that overrode the fact that they wouldn't get them once the store was closed.

"Yeah, but if there's no one here to take care of all that ..."

"Best make a sign," he said after another delay. "Going out of business."

"What will I say when someone asks why?"

"That I'm retiring."

"When?" A cold feeling settled in my stomach with that, but I kept my chin up and looked right at Sam.

"End of the month." This time there was no hesitation, no pause for him to think.

A glance at the calendar told me that it was the fourteenth of August. There were seventeen days left in the month. I swallowed hard, went to the counter, got out a sheet of paper and wrote "Store Closing August 31st" on it. I taped it up on the inside of the front door, facing out.

The questions started right away. Everyone who came into the shop wanted to know why it was closing. I repeated what he'd told me to say — that he'd decided to retire. No one seemed to notice anything unusual, even though I was sure my voice sounded hollow and false.

"You puttin' the place up for sale, Sam?" one old-timer asked.

"She'll probably sell later," he said.

"You called the store 'she,'" I commented after the man had left, "like it's a woman or something."

"Never had a wife." Sam shrugged. "Suppose this place has been the closest thing."

"Ever think about getting married?" I asked casually, remembering what Rhonda had told me about him dating my grandma. I was sure he'd tell me it was none of my business and it surprised me when he answered.

"Once. Too slow though. 'Nother fellow stepped in. *I* sent her off, though." He sounded smug and satisfied at the last comment.

I didn't push it any further, though I'd been hoping he might come right out and say something that would have told me if the woman he was talking about was my grandmother. Anyway, by his last statement, it seemed he wanted to think he'd been the one to ditch her, not the other way around. That contradicted what he'd already said, but I guess, even after all those years, a man has his pride.

The door was opening then, and Jeff Walker came in. I felt my face getting red, which was ridiculous.

"G'day, Cole," he smiled. "What's with the sign?"

"Sam's retiring," I said automatically.

"That's bad news for Kesno," Jeff said, turning toward Sam. "I reckon you've earned it though. Have any big retirement plans?"

"No," Sam said shortly. Then a smile played on the corner of his mouth. "Might take a little trip though."

He grinned outright at that. "Hope to go north, but could end up going south."

"Most folks would rather go south," Jeff pointed out as he paid for the oil and spark plugs he'd brought to the counter. "Warmer weather and all."

"Little *too* warm for my taste." Sam winked at me.

"You have a weird sense of humour," I said, as the door closed behind Jeff. I couldn't help laughing, though, and once I got started, I couldn't stop.

Sam was chuckling too, which sent him into a fit of coughing. In a moment, he was doubled over, gasping and grimacing.

I got him a glass of water and snagged the pill bottle from his pocket. As soon as he'd gotten himself under control, he swallowed a couple of pills and sat back waiting for them to kick in.

"No way to live, this," he said. His eyes were on me, and for the first time I saw something different there. It struck me that they were pleading, like he needed me to say I understood and agreed with what he was going to do.

"No, I don't suppose it is." I barely got the words out, but I think they sounded convincing.

CHAPTER TWENTY-EIGHT

"What?"

Mom looked at me with no small amount of exasperation.

"Where on earth is your head, Cole? I've asked you a question twice now, and you're just staring off into space. You've hardly touched your dinner, either."

"Asked me what?" I said. The truth was, now that I knew about how long it was going to be before Sam put his plan into place, I was having a hard time thinking about anything else.

"I was just wondering," she reached for the broccoli, "about that girl."

"What girl?"

"The girl who's been calling you."

"What about her?" I glanced at Dad, hoping he'd stop her, but he was preoccupied cutting up his ham steak.

"She hasn't called this week, has she?"

"I guess not." There was no guesswork involved. I'd been hoping Rhonda might call again, but she hadn't.

"Cole has a girlfriend," Jessie squealed. She followed this up with loud kissing sounds and giggles.

"Knock it off, Jess," I said.

"Wasn't me." Her face went innocent. "Penelope said it."

"Did you have a fight?" Mom broke in.

"Cole has a girlfriend, Cole has a girlfriend," Jessie chanted. "Cole has ..."

"Jessie! Stop that and eat your vegetables." Mom turned to me again, her face inquiring. "Well?"

"No, we didn't have a fight," I snapped. "We're just friends. Do you have to make a big deal of everything?"

"Watch your tone of voice with your mother," Dad said. Nice time for him to get involved in the conversation.

"Sorry," I mumbled.

"Because I was thinking," Mom went on, "that if you had a fight or something, you might want to call her."

"If I had a fight with someone, I'd hardly want to call them."

"Well, sometimes these things get blown out of proportion, and the best thing to do is talk it over before it's too late."

I didn't answer.

"So?"

"So, what?"

"Do you think you might go ahead and give her a call?"

It was obvious that she wasn't going to stop nagging until I agreed, so I shrugged and said I might. Mom looked satisfied and proud of herself, and I thought she'd drop the whole thing then. I shouldn't have underestimated her ability to be nosy.

"Your father and I were wondering when we might meet this young lady."

I looked at Dad to see his reaction to being dragged into this, knowing full well he'd expressed no such desire. He was pretending to be oblivious to the whole thing.

"Me an' Penelope want to meet her too," Jessie chimed in.

"Maybe you'd like to invite her to dinner one evening," Mom suggested.

"So you can interrogate her, and Jessie can torture her with that stupid doll?" I stood up and took my plate to the sink. "No thanks."

"Cole called Penelope stupid," Jessie said indignantly, like Mom hadn't heard it for herself.

"Now, Jessie, he didn't mean it. He's just upset. Lovers' quarrels will do that."

"I'll do my chores later," I said, thinking I'd better get out of the kitchen before I lost my mind.

Once I was in my room, though, I thought maybe Mom's suggestion about me phoning Rhonda wasn't so bad after all. Not for the reason she thought, but because maybe Rhonda was waiting for me to make the next move. On the other hand, maybe she never wanted to hear from me again. There was only one way to find out.

I waited until after the chores were done and I had the kitchen to myself. I looked up the phone number, started to dial, lost my nerve, and hung up. I stood staring at the phone for a minute, called myself a coward, and forced myself to dial again, resisting the panic that almost made me hang up a second time. As it started to ring, I felt my mouth go dry.

"Hello?" her mom answered.

"Uh, hi. Is Rhonda there?" A faint hope rose in me that she wouldn't be home, which didn't make much sense.

"Just a moment please." The phone clattered against some kind of hard surface and I heard Rhonda's name being called in the background.

"Hello?"

"Hello, uh, Rhonda?" Who else would it be?

"Yes, who's this?"

"It's, uh, Cole."

"Oh, hi, uh, Cole." No enthusiasm in her voice. "Shouldn't you be hanging around someone's bedroom window?"

She sounded miffed, and it took me a few seconds to figure out what she meant. Someone must have seen me helping Lisa into her room that night, and it had gotten back to Rhonda.

"You must, uh, mean Lisa," I said quickly, hoping that would prove I had nothing to hide. "I was just helping her out, so she wouldn't get in trouble with her folks."

"Yeah?" The tone of her voice had improved a lot.

"Yeah. Anyway, that's not why I, uh, called."

Stop saying "uh," I told myself firmly.

"I was, uh, wondering if you had any, uh, plans this weekend."

"What did you have in mind?"

I took that as a good sign. At least she hadn't said she had to wash her hair or anything.

"I thought you might like to, uh, see a movie."

"Sure. That'd be good."

"Yeah? Great." Elation ran through me. "Well, I'll see you there then."

Rhonda giggled. "It might be helpful if you told me *when*. So we could, you know, both be there at the same time."

"Oh, uh, what night would be good for you?" I felt like a complete moron.

"I'm free either tomorrow or Saturday evening."

"Okay, great. Well, how about tomorrow? I'll meet you there at seven?"

"Okay." More giggling.

I said "Great" for the third time, like a talking parrot that keeps repeating the same word over and over, and hung up the phone with relief. What was it about talking to Rhonda that turned me into a babbling idiot?

Well, that didn't matter now. We had a date! I started picturing how smooth I'd be once we got there this time. I'd casually put my arm across the back of her seat as soon as we sat down. From there, everything would just fall into place.

I figured she'd probably lean over against me once my arm was behind her. That brought to mind the memory of the day she'd collided with me in the field at her place. Her hair had smelled so nice, all fresh and clean, and she'd felt soft and warm. It was funny that I'd never thought of her as being pretty before that day.

Anyway, the conversation with Rhonda reminded me that I'd meant to ask Lisa how she'd managed to get Penelope back last Sunday. I gave her a call.

"Hey, Cole," she greeted me cheerfully.

I told her what I'd been wondering, thinking at the same time that she sounded okay. I was glad that she seemed to have gotten over being upset about what Wayne had done.

"It was easy," she said. "I went to the house and asked for the kid. Uh, Cassie, right? So, when she came to the door, I told her I'd heard she had a doll carriage and I wondered if I could see it, because I was thinking about getting one for some kid I knew.

"When she brought it out, I asked if I could see how many dolls it would hold, you know, so I'd know whether it was big enough or not. She went off to get some and I grabbed your sister's doll and stuffed it in the bag before she got back."

"Pretty clever," I said, though it made me a bit uncomfortable that I'd had to ask her to lie to help me out.

"So, was your sister happy to see it?"

"You have no idea."

"Well, good then. I'm glad it all worked out."

"Me too. Your folks still keeping you grounded for a whole month?"

"Looks like it," she sighed. "They said I could have friends over, though. Maybe you could come by some time."

"Okay," I said. Then, worried that she might get the wrong idea, I added, "Could I bring my girlfriend too?"

"Well, sure, but I didn't even know you were going out with anyone. Who is it?"

"Rhonda." I liked the way it felt to say her name. "Rhonda Walker."

"Cool."

"Well, actually ..." I started to explain that Rhonda and I weren't exactly, *officially*, going out. At least, not yet.

"Hey, stop that!" she yelled, interrupting me.

"Huh?" I said, startled.

"Oh, sorry. Puddles, that's my dog, was chewing on the table leg. Mom says if he ruins one more table, we're going to have to get rid of him. He's already wrecked a couple and gotten away with it, but you never know when she'll snap. That'll be the end of his chances, and of him too, I guess. Not like it would be that huge of a loss, the dumb thing. Still, I am kinda attached to him."

"Uh, look, Lisa, when I said ..."

"Puddles! Bad dog! Look, I gotta go do something with this mutt of mine. Talk to you later."

With that, she was gone. I told myself it was okay, that there was nothing to worry about, but I wasn't buying it. It wouldn't be good for Rhonda to hear that I was saying she was going out with me before I'd even asked her, and in Kesno, there's no way she wasn't going to hear it.

I figured the only thing I could do was ask her when I saw her the next night.

CHAPTER TWENTY-NINE

Word that Sam's Shop was closing its doors had gotten around fast. We were swamped on Friday, and at times, there were even queues of customers waiting to make purchases or order parts. As for repairs, Sam had started to turn folks away because he already had as much as he'd be able to handle for the next couple of weeks.

A few men asked Sam if he'd consider doing repairs from his home once the store was no longer open.

"Retired is retired," he'd say. "Try young Richardson."

"Young Richardson" is actually a fellow in his fifties. A few years ago, when a bum leg had forced him to leave his job at the mill, he'd taken a course in small engine repair and hung out a sign. Folks were used to Sam, though, and trusted his expertise, even if they found him unpleasant, so Richardson never got very busy. It looked as though business would be picking up for him soon, though.

"Think we should have a sale?" Sam asked when there was finally a lull in the middle of the afternoon. "Clear out of some of this stock?"

"I don't know," I said. "We'd be real busy then, for sure. Maybe you'd rather have things quiet for the next few weeks."

"I s'pose you're right," he agreed. "I hadn't thought of that."

I wondered then, for the first time, what was going to happen to all the stuff that was left in the shop, after Sam was gone. Or the shop itself, for that matter.

I knew Sam had a sister who'd married a fellow from Maine and gone to live in the States. It seemed likely that he'd leave the place to her, and any kids she had, but that would mean the store would probably be sold. I felt that was the right thing too. It would be strange to have someone else take over the business and keep it running.

Around four-thirty, I started watching the clock, thinking of my upcoming date with Rhonda. I hadn't thought I was being obvious about it, but Sam noticed.

"Got plans?" he asked, with the first bit of sparkle in his eyes I'd seen in a while.

"Yeah, I have a date tonight," I said, surprised at how easy it was to tell him. "I'm going to a movie with Rhonda Walker. That's Jeff's daughter."

"Nice girl?"

"She's different from other girls I know. Rhonda's real natural or something, not always going on foolish about dumb things, like clothes and rock stars and nail polish and stuff. She's fun, too."

I told him about the day she'd tricked me with the story about the rabid wolves, and Sam had a good laugh over that. I wished I had more stories to tell that would make him laugh that way.

No long after that, he announced that he was tired and had decided to close up early. It was only about quarter after five, and I knew full well he was just making an excuse so I could leave to get ready for the date with Rhonda. I didn't say anything, though, because I figured that would only embarrass him. Besides, it would give me time to eat and shower without having to rush too much.

Once I'd made sure he was safely home and had elicited a promise that he'd eat a decent dinner, I hurried to my house. I got cleaned up first, and even shaved, though it wasn't exactly necessary. Still, it gave me an excuse to put on a bit of aftershave, which I noticed made me seem a lot more mature somehow.

As usual, "Penelope" — via Jessie — made a lot of demands while we were eating. She also made a couple of rude remarks about me being smelly, which were followed by loud kissing noises and giggles. I ignored them.

"Are you doing anything tonight, dear?" Mom asked. Naturally.

"Going to the show," I said. I gave her a pleading look to drop it, with a quick nod in Jessie's direction to make my point. Amazingly, Mom smiled, nodded back, and didn't start in on the questions I knew she was dying to ask. If she got the chance, she'd corner me in private later, but I meant to get out of the house before that could happen.

As a result, I got to the theatre fifteen minutes early. That was when I realized my mistake. You see, we have a small theatre, the kind that only has one movie at time. Normally, it's changed every Thursday, but sometimes, if it's a big hit, they'll keep it for two or even three weeks. I hadn't thought to check, and was dismayed to see the "Held Over" sign up.

"Is this the same movie that was here last week?" I asked the girl at the box office, just in case the sign was wrong.

"Yeah, it's supposed to be really good," she said, like she was reciting something. "You want a ticket?"

"Uh, no. I saw it last week," I mumbled. She gave me a queer look, obviously wondering why I'd had to ask, if I'd already seen it. I wasn't about to admit that I'd been concentrating so hard on trying to hold a girl's hand that I hadn't actually noticed much of the movie.

I went outside, wondering what to do when Rhonda got there and found out what a dolt I was, inviting her to the same movie we'd watched a week ago. Their truck pulled up a few moments later, and I hurried over before Jeff could leave.

"Hey, uh, how are you?"

"Fine," she smiled, looking puzzled that I'd rushed over like that.

"There's a bit of a problem," I said, and explained about the show.

"Well, did you have something else in mind?" Jeff leaned forward to ask this, and it seemed his voice had lost its usual friendliness. If he was thinking I was planning to take Rhonda off somewhere and seduce her, he could have stopped worrying. I mean, I think about stuff like that, don't get me wrong, but I sure wasn't turning out to be some big Casanova by any means. If he'd known I hadn't even screwed up the courage to kiss her, he would have realized I wasn't much of a threat along those lines.

"We could go to The Junction," I said, "or bowling." Neither of these really appealed to me much. The Junction is always crowded, and bowling isn't what you'd call romantic, but there isn't much else to do in Kesno.

"We'll figure something out," Rhonda said firmly, stepping out of the truck. "Just let me know what time you'll be picking me up, and where."

Jeff didn't look happy, but, strangely enough, he didn't argue with her. He said how about nine, she rolled her eyes and said eleven, then they negotiated and agreed on ten-thirty.

When I heard that, I was suddenly glad we couldn't see a movie after all. It was turning out that I'd have a lot more time with her. Surely, I could make a move in three and a half hours!

Chapter Thirty

Rhonda turned to me and smiled shyly after her father had driven off. I grinned back, gawking like an idiot while we just stood there. After a moment of this, it occurred to me that maybe she was waiting for me to say something.

"So, where would you like to go?"

"I don't know," she said. "The Junction is kind of boring, and I'm not very good at bowling."

"Me neither." I'd been picturing her kicking my butt at bowling, so this was a relief.

"I guess we have to do *something* though. My dad will ask me where we went, and he won't be impressed if I have to tell him we just hung around town."

"Are you hungry?" I thought hopefully of suggesting that we go get a bite to eat. Not at Tessa's, which is about as romantic as the school gymnasium, but at Chez Pierre, the only fancy place to eat in town. I'm not sure why it was called Chez Pierre, since the owner is a woman named Margie. Maybe she thought that was a fancy sounding name.

I started picturing the two of us sitting across the table in candlelight, and how easy it would be to ask her if she wanted to go out — officially — in an atmosphere like that.

"Cole?"

"Huh?"

"I said I just ate." Rhonda looked at me curiously, and I realized she was repeating herself. I guess I'd drifted off and hadn't heard her the first time.

"Oh, yeah. Well, what would you like to do?"

"We could rent a movie and watch it at your house."

Images flashed through my head of Jessie going on foolish, which is the only way Jessie ever goes on, and Mom hovering over us like some kind of carrion eater waiting for its next meal to expire. As horrified as I was at the thought of taking Rhonda to my place, I couldn't think of an excuse, and I wasn't about to tell her how nutty my family is.

"Uh, I don't know," I said lamely.

"It will be fun," she was clearly warming to the idea. "Do you think your folks would mind?"

"No, but, uh …" I couldn't very well say they'd mind me taking her there. That would make them sound mean or something.

"Okay, then, let's do that."

So it was settled. The three and a half hours I'd been so happy about spending with her only moments before had suddenly turned into plenty of time for disaster. We walked to the video store, and I tried to concentrate as Rhonda went from title to title, pausing to read the backs of a few and asking me if I'd seen this one or that one.

"How about this?"

I pretended to be interested in the video she was holding out toward me, but the truth was I hardly saw it.

"It's a comedy."

"Yeah, okay."

"Try not to sound so enthusiastic," Rhonda frowned.

"No, I mean, it looks fine." I forced a smile, though I'm pretty sure it came out lopsided.

After I'd paid the rental charge, I suggested we stop to pick up some snacks. At that moment in time, the thought of munchies nearly made me want to heave, but at least it would delay us getting to my place. She agreed. I took as long as possible looking over the chips and stuff, until Rhonda started to look impatient. When I couldn't stall any longer, I grabbed a bag of barbeque chips and a Pepsi.

The woman at the cash smiled at us, one of those knowing adult smiles that make you feel like a little kid getting approval. Rhonda smiled back as if they were sharing a secret. For some reason, that annoyed me.

I was in a foul mood and doing my best to hide it by the time we got to my house. The minute we walked through the door, Mom appeared.

"Well, hello there," she waited expectantly, looking at Rhonda.

"This is Rhonda Walker," I mumbled. "Rhonda, this is my mom."

They greeted each other politely, then I told Mom we were going to watch a movie and asked if she could keep Jessie out of the living room.

"You're *mean*," Jessie said, coming along right on cue.

"Now, Jessie," Mom said mildly. Big help.

"Me an' Penelope wanna watch the movie *too*," Jessie said, her voice louder than usual, which is already plenty loud.

"Is this Penelope?" Rhonda asked, leaning down to inspect the doll.

"Uh-huh," Jessie said proudly. "Penelope *loves* to watch movies."

"Then Penelope can certainly watch the movie with us, can't she Cole?"

Of course, that gave me no choice but to agree. Jessie smirked, all smug and triumphant. I felt like smacking her.

"Maybe *you'd* like to see it too, Mom," I said, with no effort to keep the sarcasm out of my voice. "Heck, get Dad too, and see if the neighbours want to come over."

"There's no need to act like that, Cole," Mom said, then turned to Rhonda. "He's usually such a *nice* boy."

Now isn't that just exactly what a guy wants to hear? His mother telling his girlfriend (well, almost) that he's a nice boy!

The evening was unfolding in the disastrous way I'd expected from the first mention Rhonda had made of coming here, and it was about to get worse. When the three of us, four if you count the stupid doll, made our way to the living room, Jessie flopped on the loveseat and patted the cushion beside her.

"Penelope wants you to sit with us," she told Rhonda.

Rhonda didn't even hesitate. She smiled like that was the best idea she'd heard in a long time and went right over to sit down. I stuck the movie into the VCR, hoping it would malfunction, then dropped onto the couch. Alone.

The VCR worked just fine, which goes to show that even machines were against me on this particular occasion. Before long, Jessie and Rhonda were laughing, reminding me that it was a comedy, though I was too steamed to get into it. Once in a while, Rhonda would glance over at me and smile. I couldn't figure out how she was enjoying herself, and finally decided she'd been only too glad not to be left alone with me.

It was past nine-thirty when the movie ended, and Mom came along to send Jessie to bed. Mercifully.

"Penelope wants a kiss goodnight," Jessie said, holding the doll out.

"Goodnight, Penelope," Rhonda leaned down to comply with the insane request, then gave Jessie a kiss on the cheek too. Nice. My sister had gotten a kiss from her, but I hadn't.

"You too, Cole," Jessie smirked.

"I'm *not* kissing your dumb doll."

"See!" Her eyes shone with evil. "I *told* you he's mean."

"I'm sure he's not really," Rhonda said.

"Yes he is. One time …"

"That's enough, Jessie," Mom scooted her along. "Off to bed now."

Now that we were finally alone, all I wanted was for the evening to end. I was in the worst mood ever.

"She's sweet, isn't she?"

"Huh? You mean Jessie?"

"Yeah, she's really cute."

"Oh, adorable," I said bitterly.

"You didn't really mind her watching the movie with us, did you?"

I shrugged. There was no way I was going to agree, and telling the truth probably wasn't the best idea.

"Anyway, I suppose we should walk back to the theatre. Dad's picking me up there at ten-thirty," she reminded me.

As we made our way along the street, I thought that this would definitely be the last date I ever had with Rhonda. It seemed as though she'd been part of a conspiracy to ruin the whole night.

"Maybe you can come out to my place this Sunday."

"Maybe."

"I mean, I thought you might like to come over, seeing as how we're going out and all."

I'd forgotten all about my plan to ask her out officially. Her remark, tossed out so casually, made it clear that she'd heard about what I'd told Lisa.

"Look, I, uh ..." I stammered, embarrassed and caught off guard.

"It's okay, you know." She reached out and touched my hand. "I didn't mind."

Just like that I forgot about how mad I'd been and how I'd decided, only moments before, that I wasn't going to see her again.

"So, you *will* go out with me?" I grinned at her like an idiot.

"I thought I already was," she teased. Then her smile faded, and she moved a little closer. "Yes," she breathed softly, "I'll go out with you."

Without stopping to work up the nerve or think about it or anything, I finally kissed her.

Chapter Thirty-one

You know how it is on the last day of school every June, when you have the whole summer stretching out ahead of you and it seems as if it will last forever? Then the next thing you know, it's almost over, and you're counting the days, dreading the thought of giving up all that glorious freedom to sit in a stuffy classroom day after day.

Not that I mind school, really. Never have. Still, I always feel kind of sorry to go back after the holidays.

This year, though, it wasn't the thought of school that was uppermost in my mind as August drew to a close. Every day that went by reminded me that Sam was that much closer to death. I imagine he was thinking about it a good deal too, but he never mentioned the subject again. I figured he didn't want to talk about it, so I didn't bring it up either, though there were things I really wanted to ask him.

For one thing, I wondered if he believed in an afterlife. Then there was the whole matter of whether or not what he was going to do was wrong, from a religious point of view. From what I've heard in church, folks don't have the right to decide that, it's supposed to be up to God.

But, maybe it's different to kill yourself if you're dying anyway, than if you just decide you don't want to live because you feel depressed or something. I mean, if there's no hope that you'll get better and all that lies ahead is suffering, does that create some kind of loophole in the rules? I didn't think so, but then I didn't know for sure.

I had no one to talk to about all this, and that made it even harder. On the other hand, I already knew what my folks, or our pastor, would say if I brought the subject up. Some things are pretty black and white to most people. In a way, I wished I could be like that too. It might not be a comfort, but at least I wouldn't feel confused.

I almost talked to Rhonda about it, but stopped myself at the last minute. It occurred to me, just as I was about to bring it up, that she'd think it was a pretty strange topic, and it might alarm her. For sure she'd wonder why I wanted to discuss suicide, and I knew she'd press for the reason. I wasn't sure I'd be able to keep the secret from her; she has this certain look that can really weaken a guy's resolve.

All told, it had been a pretty strange summer. So many unexpected things had happened, like getting the job with Sam, discovering that I was interested in Rhonda, and seeing a lifelong friendship crumble.

Speaking of Wayne, I'd run into him a couple of times since the day I'd told him off, and I noticed that my attitude toward him had softened. Not that I wanted to go back to being bossed around and ridiculed, but it seemed that there should be *something* worth keeping from a friendship that had lasted all those years. I thought that even though we might not hang out the way we used to, we didn't have to be enemies either.

Apparently, Wayne didn't feel that way. Both times I'd seen him, I'd said "Hi" in a casual, friendly way. I won't repeat what he'd said in return. But then, when Wayne gets mad, he stays that way. He has a kind of all or nothing approach to things. As he used to say, "My way or the highway."

I was kind of surprised to find that it didn't really bother me — I didn't feel like it was some big loss or anything. In fact, I was sort of relieved; it was settled and that was that.

I have to admit that, even though I have a girl-friend now, it left me feeling sort of adrift. A guy needs another guy to hang out with, someone he can talk to about stuff that matters. I didn't spend too much time worrying about it, though. It's not as if I don't have other friends, so I figured I'd eventually end up being best buds with one of them.

Anyway, Sam and Rhonda were pretty much taking up all the spare time I had at the moment. I spent an hour or so at Sam's house every day, just kind of helping him out with things and trying to make sure he was eating. That was getting to be more and more of a challenge.

Sam kind of made fun of me over that, and asked me stuff like did I think a chicken dinner might cure him, and was I his mom or what? I guess his attitude was that since he wasn't going to be around for long, it didn't make much difference if he took care of himself in the meantime.

I couldn't argue with that, but deep inside I was hoping he might change his mind, in which case it *would* matter. Once, I kind of hinted that he didn't have to go through with his plan.

"Why not?" he asked, shifting awkwardly in his chair.

I didn't have an answer for that. Then he went on.

"For *whose* sake would you like me to stick around?"

I got the point right away. I hadn't been thinking of Sam, I'd been thinking of myself, and what I wanted. Not what was best for him, though, as I've said, I wasn't exactly clear on what that might happen to be.

Then, before I knew it, the thirty-first of August had arrived. The last day for Sam's Shop to be open, and possibly the last time I would see him alive. I could hardly get through the day.

CHAPTER THIRTY-TWO

There were a lot of thoughts racing around in my head when I accompanied Sam home that day. You'd think there'd be any number of things a person might say at a time like that, but Sam's silence didn't invite conversation. It was like an unspoken command hung in the air, forbidding words.

We went into the house, went through the ritual of me doing what I could to make him comfortable before I tidied up a bit. I kept seeing more and more things that should be taken care of before … well, before anyone came in. To take him out for the last time.

I suppose it was ridiculous to worry about how clean the place would be when whoever it is that takes out a body arrived. It's not likely that they'd even notice if the place was dusted or the floors had been cleaned. Anyway, Sam certainly wouldn't care what they thought. I don't know why I did.

He was asleep in the big easy chair in the living room when I slipped out the door, and I couldn't help picturing him there at the very end. Seemed the one spot he felt most comfortable.

I walked home, wishing I had somewhere else to go. Listening to Mom and Jessie right about then didn't appeal to me one bit. Sure enough, it started as soon as I went through the door.

"Cole loves Rhonda." Jessie set up a chant, dancing around me like some kind of trained circus animal.

"We already ate," Mom said, smiling as if Jessie's performance was cute, or amusing. "I made you a plate, but you'll have to microwave it."

She thrust a helping of shepherd's pie toward me. I took it automatically and stuck it in to heat, though I wasn't feeling one bit hungry. Jessie plopped down on the chair across from me and kept up a steady stream of annoying comments while I picked at my food. I ignored her.

After forcing down about half of it, I couldn't eat any more. Mom arched an eyebrow when she saw me scraping the remainder into the garbage.

"Is anything wrong, dear?"

I shook my head, rinsing the plate under the tap.

"You seem a bit out of sorts." As usual, she refused to drop it. "Did you and Rhonda have a fight?"

"No."

"Well, something's obviously bothering you."

"Yeah, *you're* bothering me, and *Jessie's* bothering me," I almost yelled. Suddenly, I realized that tears were swelling up in my eyes. I knew I had to get out of there.

"I'll do my chores later," I said, half choking on the words as I fled out the back door.

As soon as my feet hit the sidewalk I started running. It was as if I had to get as far away as I could, only I wasn't sure from what. I ran until my sides hurt, finally stopping to catch my breath at the quarry. There, I collapsed on the ground, panting and bawling like a little kid. I was glad no one was around to see it.

I'm not sure how long I lay there. Time seemed to kind of stand still, like there was only one huge moment that never ended, and I was suspended in it. Things were whirling around in my brain, thoughts zipping in and out, connecting to others then slipping away. I wondered if this was how people went mad.

Eventually, it all calmed and settled, leaving me exhausted, as if I hadn't slept in weeks. I finally gathered the energy to get back up, dragging myself to my feet like a rag doll, and started for home.

Only, I didn't end up at home. Without even thinking about it, I found myself at Sam's door. The lights were on inside, but I knew that didn't mean anything. He could be sleeping, or ... With the half-formed thought that he might already be gone, I found panic and, for some strange reason, anger welling inside me. I pounded on the door, calling his name.

"Cole?" His grizzled face appeared a moment later. He looked like he'd just woken up.

"Yeah." I guess I didn't sound too friendly.

"What is it?"

"What is it? What do you mean, what is it?" I realized I was shouting, took a breath, and continued in as normal a voice as I could manage. "I came to see you, that's all."

"Well, come in then."

I followed him into the living room, plunked down on the couch, and took a deep breath, trying to calm the shaking inside.

"You're not even going to say goodbye, are you?"

He didn't answer. *Just like the good old days*, I thought.

"It's not right, you know. It's not fair."

"Lots of things in life aren't fair," he said.

"Yeah, well, you don't treat people like that. You just don't do it. Not if you care anything about them."

"Wasn't planning to." He leaned forward, wincing slightly. "Was gonna call you later."

"Well, that's great. That's real good." I couldn't seem to control my anger any more than I could explain it. I mean, there I was, talking to a man who would soon be dead, and instead of feeling bad about it, I was furious. "I guess I should feel honoured that you actually figure I deserve a phone call. That's rich!"

"You done?"

"No, I'm not done," I snapped. I was winding up to really tell him what I thought, but it hit me how small and frail and tired he looked. As quick as it had come, my anger drained away. I shrugged. "Yeah, I guess I am."

"Well, don't join the debate team at school, if that's the best you can do."

It wasn't even that funny, but I started laughing and couldn't get stopped. From crying to being mad to laughing like some kind of moron — it had been quite a day.

I finally pulled myself together, feeling a bit foolish. Sam looked at me and nodded. I didn't know what he meant by that.

"What I was going to call you for," he said at length, "was to see if you might want to come by tomorrow. Afternoon. After lunch."

I knew without him spelling it out that he was going to do it then. And I was going to be there. Right away I felt nervous and kind of scared, but at the same time, I was glad.

Sam Kerrigan wasn't going to die alone.

Chapter Thirty-three

I figured that when I got home that night I'd be in trouble for the way I'd acted earlier, but Mom never said a word to me about it. In fact, she didn't say anything at all, just went about like everything was normal. I guess I should have said I was sorry or something, but it wasn't in me at the time.

Mostly, I wanted to be left alone, so her silence was kind of a relief. I went to my room and was lying on my bed thinking about the next day when Jessie knocked, and then came barging in before I could open my mouth to tell her to go away.

"You're moody because of pimples and stuff," she announced, plopping down beside me.

"I don't have any pimples," I pointed out, wondering what she was getting at.

She peered closely at my face to see if this was true.

At the same time, she held up her dumb doll, as if it was checking too.

"But Mom said you have all these horzones and they make you get pimples and act mean sometimes."

"Hormones," I corrected.

"Yeah, horzones, an' Mom says it's not your fault, 'cause of the pimples an' everything."

"Whatever." In spite of myself, I felt a bit pleased to think Mom was standing up for me, taking my side in her own strange way. It might seem small, but at least I knew she was still paying attention, even if she is wrapped up in her soaps so often.

"Anyway, me an' Penelope aren't mad at you or nothin', 'cause you can't help it."

She reached out and patted me on the arm, apparently consoling me over this raging hormone situation that I couldn't do anything about.

"Well, uh, thanks," I said, hardly able to keep from laughing at how serious she looked. "Did Mom tell you how all these 'horzones' make a person need to be alone sometimes?"

"No, she never said nothin' about that."

"Well, they do, once in a while."

"Are the horzones doing that to you right now?" she asked solemnly.

"Yeah, kind of."

She nodded to show she understood, and slipped

down from the bed. I smiled to myself as she walked out of the room, holding her head high, obviously proud about her newfound maturity. Just when a guy is sure that all the females in his life are out to make him miserable, something like this happens. Then you know they're not so bad after all.

I don't remember falling asleep that night. Usually I feel myself drifting off and I know I'm just about gone, but not this time. The next thing I knew, it was morning, and I was lying there, still dressed from the day before.

I showered and put on clean clothes, picked at some breakfast, and straightened up my room. Rhonda called a little after ten, wanting to know if we were getting together later. I didn't quite know what to tell her, since I couldn't predict how I'd feel when the afternoon was over. I told her I'd call her around six, and we could make plans then.

All morning, I watched the clock with a mixture of impatience and dread. While I was anxious to get to Sam's, I was also acutely aware that every moment that passed was one of his last. I wondered what he was thinking and feeling.

By the time eleven-thirty had arrived I couldn't take it anymore, so I headed out for his place. I was surprised to find him sitting out on the front step. He smiled as I settled beside him, and an irrational hope rose in me that he'd changed his mind.

We sat there without speaking for a good ten minutes. It was Sam who broke the silence.

"It was a good summer."

That choked me up real quick, because I knew exactly what he was telling me. Unable to answer, I just nodded.

"I'm not one for making speeches," Sam went on after a pause. "Never much cottoned to folk who talked on and on. Still, there're some things a person *ought* to say, and it seems those things are the hardest to get out.

"I'm awful glad you came lookin' for work. You were a real help." He reached across and patted my knee. "In lotsa ways."

"You ever have a helper before?" I asked.

"Nope."

"How come?"

"Never had anyone ask for a job. Seemed to manage okay on my own anyway."

"Why'd you hire me?"

"You knew what a keel stick was." He grinned at me. "Didn't think you would. Most folks call it a lumber crayon."

"My grandpa taught me stuff like that."

"Your grandpa's a good man. Always was." There was a wistful sound to his voice as he said this, and I wondered if he was thinking about my grandmother.

It seemed he'd used up all the conversation he had at the moment, and we sat there under the warm sun without speaking any further until he announced it was time to go in.

Panic washed over me, but I shoved down the sudden urge to plead with him not to do it. I followed him inside.

When we reached the living room I could hardly believe my eyes. There, leaning on its stand, was a Kona Hardtail Stuff with a top-of-the-line helmet hanging from one handlebar.

I remembered how, some weeks back, Sam had casually asked me about the kind of bike I'd been planning to buy, and how important it had seemed to me such a short time ago.

"This the right one?" Sam asked.

"Yeah." I was too dumbstruck to say anything more.

"Good then."

"Sam, I ..." My voice choked and broke off.

"Now, enough of that." Sam's voice was husky. "There's a couple of things we need to get straight. First one's that there's to be no big display. No need to be feeling bad or anything.

"Second thing is for your protection," he continued, though the effort seemed to be wearing him out. "You don't know anything. By that, I mean, you have no part in this. Understand?"

"I think so."

"You came by because I wasn't feeling too good, and later on you saw that I was gone, and that's that. That's all you know."

"Okay."

"Otherwise, I think it could mean some kind of trouble for you. So, you're not going to see anything. I'll be doing what I need to do in private. Then, if you still want to stay, you can just sit and talk for a bit. This is just a visit, is all you know."

"All right, Sam."

"Well, then." He nodded, satisfied. "I'm thinking that I'm ready."

CHAPTER THIRTY-FOUR

Sam left me then, telling me to check out the bike and he'd be back in a few minutes. I walked around it a few times, but I really wasn't seeing it. I could hear him in the kitchen, and the sound of the tap running sent chills through me. Trying to shut it out, I sat down, put my hands over my ears, and squeezed my eyes shut, but the mental image of Sam swallowing handfuls of pills wouldn't disappear.

It occurred to me how strange it was that at the start of the summer, the bike had been the only thing on my mind, and I'd been willing to put up with Sam in order to get it. Now, I'd have gladly given it up, and lots more with it, if only he didn't have to die. I felt like kicking it to pieces, even though I knew that was stupid, and that I'd probably feel differently about it later on, since it was a gift from Sam.

"Cole?" Sam's voice cut into my thoughts. I nearly jumped right off the couch. "I believe I'll lie down for a bit now," he said.

I followed him to his room. There was a chair sitting beside his bed. I visualized him putting it there earlier in the day, getting everything ready.

Sam eased down onto the bed and lay back. I sank weakly onto the chair. Sunlight streamed through the window, falling on his tired old face. It reminded me of what he'd said a while back, about there being a light that folks go to when they die.

"I guess you'll be needing to call someone, later on," he said. "Don't call too soon, though. Make sure first."

"Okay, Sam."

As the moments ticked by, I found myself looking around the room. It was the first time I'd ever been in there, and it struck me how bare the walls were. It wasn't until my eyes had travelled all the way around the room that I saw the single picture, a five-by-seven photo in black and white, perched on the night table behind me. I peered closely at it.

A couple stood there, frozen from some day long gone, their smiles awkward and stiff. Her dress was long, but not all puffed out around the bottom, the way you think of old-fashioned dresses being. Both wore hats, hers kind of funny shaped, his the style old men wear, almost flat except for a slight rise at the back, with a wide, round peak on the front.

The man's face looked vaguely familiar, and I realized it resembled Sam, just a little.

"Are these your parents?" I asked him, picking up the picture.

He smiled. "No, that's me, and a young woman I once knew."

I knew immediately that the young woman was my grandmother. Why I hadn't realized it right away is beyond me. I guess I wasn't thinking straight.

"I was powerful fond of her." Sam's speech seemed to be coming hard, like it was a huge effort for him to get the words out. "She married another, though."

"You never found anyone else?"

"Never looked." His eyes stared off into the distance. "I guess you might know who she is, do you, son?"

"Yeah."

"She was a fine woman," he nodded, as if to back up what he was saying. "It's too bad you never knew her."

I held the picture out to him, and he took it without a word. His gnarled hand clutched the frame and he stared at it for a moment. Something soft settled over his face, then he laid it, face down, against his chest and put his hand over top of it.

"*I* sent her off," he said. There was a strange sound of satisfaction in his words. His eyes closed.

I reached over and took hold of Sam's hand. He didn't object, though I'd feared he might, so I guess it was okay with him.

"I'm glad you're here, Cole," he said in a barely audible whisper.

I clenched my teeth together hard, until my jaw hurt, determined to keep from crying. Sam didn't want that, he'd said so. I wasn't going to go against his last wishes if I could possibly help it.

He never spoke again. Before long, his breathing changed, slowing and becoming laboured. It continued that way for a while, and then his breaths were coming farther and farther apart.

I'm not sure how long it took, really. It could have been minutes or hours. I'd lost all sense of time. I only knew that I was listening hard for each rasping breath, almost holding my own, waiting for each one to arrive. And then, there were no more.

Sam Kerrigan was gone. I hoped he'd found the light and that it was warm and bright and that he had stepped into a new world where there was no pain.

I don't know how long I stayed there afterward. I think I was waiting, expecting to cry then, once he was gone, but tears didn't come. Not then.

Finally, I let go of his hand, placed it with the other one, over the picture of my grandmother. I wondered if she was where he'd gone, and if they still knew each other.

I left him. I wandered through the house, thinking about the summer and all that had happened. I knew I had to call the hospital or something, but I wasn't ready yet. It seemed there were things that I needed to let settle before I could pick up the phone.

I went back to look at Sam a few times, and it was on the last trip into his room that something came to me. Four words, their meaning lost on me at the time, echoed in my head. Then I knew.

I almost ran to the spare bedroom, where I'd piled all his ledgers a few weeks back. Doing some quick math in my head, I reached for one down low in a stack and drew it out.

I found what I was looking for when I got to the July entries. It was just a number, a large amount for the time, neatly recorded without anything further written, but it told me what I wanted to know. What I did know, but needed to confirm.

Sam Kerrigan was the man who had anonymously paid for my grandmother's funeral. It hadn't been my grandfather's boss, as he'd thought.

That was what he'd meant, both times he'd told me he'd sent her off! Of course, he'd had no reason to think I'd ever understand the real meaning behind his words.

And I knew I would keep Sam's secret, that I'd never tell anyone, not even my grandfather. It's what Sam would have wanted.

I closed the book, replaced it in the pile, stood and took a deep breath.

It was time to make a phone call.

Acknowledgements

Writing from a male perspective was a good deal of fun, but since I have never been a teenage boy, it was also a little scary and a rather unique challenge. I relied a good deal on feedback from my husband, Brent, who never fails to provide love and support.

For various other blessings, I thank, with love:

My children, Anthony and Pamela, my parents, Bob and Pauline Russell, my brothers, Danny and Andrew, their respective partners, Gail and Shelley, and the Sherrard family, for their love and encouragement.

Alf Lower, who went from teacher to friend.

Friends who are more important than they will ever know: Janet Aube, Dawn and Jacob Black, Karen Donovan, Ray Doucet, Karen Dyer, Angie Garofolo, John Hambrook, Sandra Henderson, David Jardine, Johnnye Montgomery, Marsha Skrypuch, Paul Theriault, and Bonnie Thompson.

At work: Jimmy Allain, Karen Arseneault, Ann Craik, Shelley Donahue, Julie Donovan, Eric Fallon, Sue Fitzpatrick, Andy Flanagan, Carol Forrest, Edison Jardine, Gabrielle Kennedy, Mary Matchett, Rhona Muir, Faye Nowlan, Carla O'Toole, Sarah Scott, Julia Trevors, and Beatrice Tucker.

At The Dundurn Group: Kirk Howard, Publisher, and the whole gang, especially my editor, Barry Jowett, Andrea Pruss, Jennifer Scott, and Jennifer (Queenie) Foster. Working with each of them is an honour and a pleasure.

And, finally, the young people who read, who reach a little deeper, and who connect with the voice of a story. You are on these pages and they belong to you.